THE PLOT TO KILL HITLER

BOOK TWO

EXECUTION

ANDY MARINO

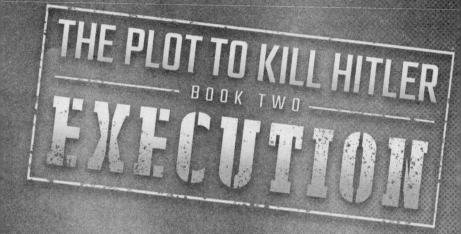

THE PLOT TO KILL HITLER

BOOK TWO

EXECUTION

ANDY MARINO

Scholastic Inc.

Copyright © 2020 by Andy Marino

All rights reserved. Published by Scholastic Inc., *Publishers since 1920.* SCHOLASTIC and associated logos are trademarks and/or registered trademarks of Scholastic Inc.

The publisher does not have any control over and does not assume any responsibility for author or third-party websites or their content.

No part of this publication may be reproduced, stored in a retrieval system, or transmitted in any form or by any means, electronic, mechanical, photocopying, recording, or otherwise, without written permission of the publisher. For information regarding permission, write to Scholastic Inc., Attention: Permissions Department, 557 Broadway, New York, NY 10012.

This book is a work of fiction. Names, characters, places, and incidents are either the product of the author's imagination or are used fictitiously, and any resemblance to actual persons, living or dead, business establishments, events, or locales is entirely coincidental.

ISBN 978-1-338-35904-6

10 9 8 7 6 5 4 3 2 1   20 21 22 23 24

First edition, May 2020

Printed in the U.S.A.   40

Book design by Christopher Stengel

For Chris

ONE

The cramped upper rooms of the two-story flat in Prenzlauer Berg baked in the summer sun. Max Hoffmann never thought he would miss frigid winter nights, but the June heat was making him nostalgic for snow, ice, and the bitter wind that howled through the streets of Berlin. He mopped sweat from his brow with the edge of a bedsheet. The humid air of the safe house smelled of mold, despite the Hoffmanns' best efforts to keep their new home clean and dry.

Max, Gerta, Mutti, Papa—all of them attacking the nooks and crannies of the dismal old flat with brooms and dust rags, scouring the washroom with what little cleaning powder they received with their meager rations, stashed weekly in the flat's overgrown backyard by the communist underground. Their benefactors might as well be ghosts. Max had never seen them.

The Hoffmanns cleaned and cleaned. The mold persisted.

Max remembered Frau Becker sliding the curtain of her car window aside to take in the view of her beloved Berlin back in February, when she had discussed plans with the Hoffmanns for exposing the Nazi spy in their midst. *Smells like rot*, she'd said. Max wondered if it wasn't just their safe house that was redolent of decay, but the city itself. The entire Third Reich positively reeked of it these days.

By now, Frau Becker was decaying, too, he thought darkly. A mound of bones in some unmarked traitor's grave—if the Nazis hadn't just thrown her corpse on the fire. The fierce old woman deserved so much better. Max felt a dizzying rush forming in the pit of his stomach. He sat cross-legged on his narrow cot with his back against the wall and clenched the thin sheet in his fists. He bunched up the fabric as if holding on tight could anchor him against what was about to happen. The wall across from his bed was no more than three or four paces away, but as dizziness took hold, the small room seemed to stretch out in front of him and the wall hazed into some unreal distance. It was as if he were looking through a telescope in reverse. Pins and needles shot down into his legs and prickled his chest as a peculiar weightlessness took hold.

His knuckles turned white as he clung to the sheet and gritted his teeth. This was what happened when he thought too much about the Becker Circle's demise. He was rocketed along at a million kilometers per hour, propelled by a deep and terrible sense of the sheer *unfairness* of it all. It was a sensation like nothing he had ever known.

It wasn't fair that Hans Meier, the person he had liked

best in the Becker Circle, turned out to be a Nazi spy.

It wasn't fair that Frau Becker never got to see the Nazi flags torn down in the city that she loved.

It wasn't fair that Max, Gerta, Mutti, and Papa had been forced to leave their old lives behind and trade their airy villa in Dahlem for a smelly, old row house in Prenzlauer Berg, where they weren't even allowed to go outside.

It wasn't fair that Herr Trott and General Vogel had been executed, and Albert and Princess Marie had vanished without a trace.

Finally, it wasn't fair that Adolf Hitler was alive and Frau Becker was dead. That alone was proof that the universe was tilted in favor of evil over good.

The room spun. Max felt like he was in free fall, a pilot ejected from a burning plane without a parachute. Fragments of winter nights danced madly in his head—death in the shadows of the ruined opera house, wet chalk on blackened brick . . .

"Stop stop stop stop stop," Max said. If he didn't pull himself back to reality, this little episode would leave him feeling awful for the rest of the day.

He closed his eyes and tried to blank his mind. A few weeks ago, after an episode at the dinner table, Papa had taught him breathing exercises to help keep him tethered to the real world when his body and mind started to spin out of his control. He inhaled to a count of five and exhaled to a count of seven, the whole time thinking *sloooowwww dowwwwnnnnnn*, stretching the word like a piece of toffee in his mind.

After several long, slow breaths, he risked opening his eyes. The wall had returned to its proper place. He let go of the bedsheet and sat perfectly still for a moment, thinking: *calm.*

He focused on sounds from other parts of the flat: Mutti and Papa puttering around downstairs, sipping weak ersatz coffee and munching on stale bread. Gerta and Kat Vogel talking quietly in their room across the narrow hallway.

Here was another fine example of the unfairness of it all: Now that they'd moved to a much smaller house, Max had to share it with not one older girl, but *two.*

He knew it was a horribly selfish thought. Kat's father had been executed by the Nazis, her mother sent to a camp in Poland. Kat herself had narrowly escaped the same fate. He was glad that she was alive. But couldn't she be alive somewhere else?

There was barely enough food for the four Hoffmanns, and most everything came with substitute ingredients—sawdust instead of flour, roasted grain instead of coffee beans. They weren't starving, but they had all lost a little bit of weight. Max's hunger was a small bright pebble in his stomach, always there to remind him that he was surviving on scraps.

It was time to go downstairs and force down a slice of dry, mealy bread for breakfast.

He decided he would wait until Gerta and Kat went down, ate, and came back up to their room. He didn't feel like talking to anyone this morning. To pass the time, he thumbed through one of the French theatrical programs some previous occupant of the safe house had left in a pile in the corner of the bedroom. Since the Hoffmanns had arrived at the house in February, Max had actually managed to teach himself to read a little bit of French, but today he just let the words of *Le Coeur Dispose* wash over him.

A bead of sweat fell from the tip of his nose and splatted against the program, splotching the print. Max tossed the booklet aside and mopped his forehead with the sheet.

It was hard to imagine a time when he had ever been cold. He hugged his arms to his chest and tried to make himself shiver, as if he could lower the temperature by memory alone.

Suddenly, footsteps pounded up the stairs. Max hopped out of bed in alarm—the whole family was supposed to tread lightly in the safe house. Mutti appeared in his doorway, wide-eyed and breathless.

"It's begun!" she said. Then she turned and poked her head into Gerta and Kat's room. "Get up, get up, they've finally done it!"

"Done what?" Max said, going out into the hall. His mother took him by the shoulders and laughed.

"They've just announced it on the radio!"

Max was stunned by this abrupt burst of energy. His family had been moping around the house for weeks, barely speaking, and now it seemed as if Mutti had gone mad.

"The Allies have landed in France!"

TWO

The radio in the safe house was an old Volksempfänger, manufactured before the war. Its Bakelite plastic cabinet was scuffed and chipped, and the brown fabric that covered the speaker was peeling off. It picked up German stations well enough, but BBC broadcasts came through weak and patchy. The Hoffmanns sat as close as they possibly could, and Max found himself holding his breath so as not to miss a word.

Listening to the British reports—along with *Hornet and Wasp*, his favorite BBC serial program—throughout the war had given Max a basic grasp of the English language, but the radio's poor reception tested his abilities. Papa, who spoke English and French fluently, along with little bits of Hungarian and Czech, translated the broadcaster's words for the family.

"D-Day has come," Papa said, his ear pressed against the speaker cover. "Early this morning the Allies began the assault on the northwestern face of Hitler's European Fortress."

D-Day, Max thought. To think that just a few minutes ago he'd been preparing himself for another boring morning in the safe house . . .

"Under the command of General Eisenhower," Papa continued, "Allied naval forces supported by strong air forces began landing Allied armies on the northern coast of France. This army group includes British, Canadian, and United States forces."

Max tried to picture the northern coast of France. He knew that Hitler's Atlantic Wall, composed of cement pillboxes and bunkers bristling with heavy guns, stretched up and down the beaches for hundreds of miles. The Allied ships would have to unload their troops at the shoreline, and the men would have to fight their way up the beaches, exposed and vulnerable, while the Germans cut them down from the shelter of their fortifications. It was going to be a bloodbath.

"Here's a statement from General Eisenhower," Papa said. "'Your task will not be an easy one. Your enemy is well trained, well equipped, and battle hardened. He will fight savagely. But this is the year 1944. The tide has turned. The free men of the world are marching together to victory.'"

Mutti nudged Papa. "See what the German broadcasts are saying, Karl."

"Probably nothing," Gerta said.

"Probably, *the Allies have fallen right into Hitler's brilliant trap*," Kat Vogel said. Max glanced at their "houseguest." When

Kat had first moved in with them back in February, he had tried to pick up some hint of General Vogel in her features, to no avail. He figured she must take after her mother, because in Kat there was no trace of the round face, slightly bulging eyes, and well-fed plumpness of the blustery military man. This was probably for the best—imagining a thirteen-year-old girl with General Vogel's features was a bit unsettling. Instead, Kat was fine-boned and long-limbed. She lounged about in a way that reminded Max of a skinny bug, like a praying mantis, folding her arms and legs as if they hinged on three joints instead of two. Her eyes were bright and searching, and she had a nervous habit of tapping out rhythms that only she could hear on her knees and the safe house's shabby furniture.

Papa turned the dial to a German-language news broadcast.

To Max's surprise, the newscaster was actually announcing the Allied invasion.

"A battle for life and death is in progress," the newscaster said. "Early this morning, American, Canadian, and British forces landed on the coast of France, from Cherbourg to Le Havre, preceded by large naval bombardments. They have now penetrated several kilometers between Caen and Isigny. Our forces are bringing reinforcements up the coast."

Papa turned the dial to another German news broadcast. This one was more strident, and Max thought the report must have come straight from the propaganda minister himself.

"The combined might of the Allied forces are smashing

themselves to pieces against the fire and steel of Field Marshal Rommel's impenetrable Atlantic Wall! The Wehrmacht has repelled the first wave of the invasion, and expects to send the Allied fleet back across the Channel by nightfall."

There was a burst of static as Papa switched the dial back to the BBC. Mutti disappeared into the flat's tiny kitchen and reappeared a moment later carrying a tin of black-market biscuits. She handed one to Max, Gerta, Kat, and Papa in turn, then bit into one herself.

"I didn't know we had biscuits," Max said.

Papa smiled. "We have been saving them for a special occasion."

Max took a small bite, savoring the taste of real sugar and butter. The communists had dropped off some ersatz biscuits last week, and they had tasted like pulped wood. These were the real thing, with actual flavor. He grinned at Gerta, who was chewing the entire biscuit at once. She stuck out her crumb-covered tongue and he feigned total disgust. Then he noticed that Kat was holding her biscuit uneaten in her lap, sitting cross-legged on the floor, staring balefully at the radio as the BBC newscaster announced that His Majesty the King would address the nation later that day.

Her hand darted up to the dial and she switched the radio off.

"How far is it?" Kat said.

"How far is what?" Papa said.

"From the place where the Allies landed in France to Berlin."

"I'm not sure," Papa admitted. "A thousand kilometers at least. Probably more."

"A thousand kilometers," Kat said quietly. "And first they will have to go to Paris, I guess."

"Yes," Mutti said. "First the Allies will liberate Paris."

"How long will it take them to get here?" Kat said.

"I don't know," Papa said.

Kat got to her feet. "Weeks?" she said, her voice rising in pitch. "Months? *Years?*"

"He said he didn't know," Gerta said. "Put the radio back on, Kat."

"I can't just sit around this place waiting for them!" Kat crushed her biscuit in her hand as she made a fist and pounded it against her hip.

"Can't you just be happy for two minutes?" Max blurted out. "The Allies are coming! They've actually landed! It's what we've been wanting this whole time."

Kat stalked over to Max. He took a step back.

"Do you know what I want, Max?" she said. There was a fierce twist to her face. "I want to see my mother again. I want her to *live*. And by the time the damned Allies get here, the Nazis will have killed everyone in the camps. So don't tell me to be happy!"

With that, Kat stomped upstairs. Max heard the door slam and the creak of springs as she threw herself down on the bed.

His face felt hot. It seemed like he could never say the right thing around Kat. She could go from playful and giddy to raging and depressed in the blink of an eye.

"I'll go talk to her," Gerta said, heading upstairs.

"I'm sorry," Max said.

"Kat has lost so much," Mutti said quietly. "You must try to imagine what it's like for her to be around us all the time—a family that is by the grace of God still together."

"I know," Max said. "I'm just excited about the news."

"So am I, Maxi," Papa said, turning the radio back on. "So am I."

THREE

Kat hasn't said a word to me," Gerta whispered. "She's just moping around."

Gerta was sitting on the only other piece of furniture in Max's bedroom: a rickety wooden chair. It was the day after the Allies landed, and the news was mixed: According to the BBC, the Allies had taken casualties but had not been forced off any of the landing beaches. Some troops were beginning to move inland, but the beachheads were still isolated. Papa urged patience: The Wehrmacht was well fortified, after all. It would take time for the Allies to sweep them off the Atlantic Wall. But the important thing was that the Allies held the beaches, so they could unload the vast amounts of men and equipment they would need to begin their march across occupied France.

"Don't look at me," Max said quietly. "I always say the wrong thing to her."

Gerta considered this. "You really do. It's like a special skill of yours—Hornet can pick any lock, Wasp never backs down from a fight, Max Hoffmann has no tact."

"I didn't mean anything by it," Max insisted. "I just wanted us all to be happy, for once." He sipped tepid water from a glass and made a face. Berlin hadn't been bombed in several weeks—the RAF was focused on striking Nazi positions in France—but Max could still taste a hint of ash in the water. He handed the glass to Gerta, who drained it and set it down on the floor beside the chair.

"Yum," she said. "Bomb water."

"Fresh from the mountain streams."

Nobody laughed. Their jokes were as stale as the air in the safe house. If not for the relief of the D-Day interruption, they probably would have descended into silence for days. He went to the room's single small window and moved the curtain aside. His bedroom faced the street, so he was forbidden to open his curtain all the way. When he peeked out, he had to be careful not to attract attention.

The view wasn't much. He scanned the midday street. A few Berliners passed by on their way to the market. There was a decent grocery store at the end of the block, but the Hoffmanns could never shop there. Only Papa had been able to get forged identification documents, and he never left the safe house during the day. It had been several months since the Becker Circle was betrayed, but the Gestapo wasn't known for letting traitors slip away. They would not rest until all the conspirators—and their families—had been rounded up.

Max let the curtain fall back into place and turned to his sister.

"Do you think Colonel Stauffenberg is still alive?"

Over the past few months, Max had often found himself thinking of the tall aristocrat. He had only met the man once, when Stauffenberg had visited Frau Becker's sitting room, but the memory was etched in his mind. Sometimes, when he sensed a dizzy spell coming on, Max pictured Stauffenberg striding confidently into the room, radiating energy and resourcefulness despite his terrible injuries.

Inviting Max, with a twinkle in his good eye, to commit high treason with him.

"I don't know," Gerta said. "I guess it depends on whether Hans gave him up or not."

After General Vogel's execution and Kat's narrow escape, news had trickled in through the communist underground about Herr Trott's arrest and the disappearance of Albert and the princess. But the Hoffmanns had not received any word about the Becker Circle's military counterparts. Even Papa did not seem to have any idea if the plot to kill Hitler had been abandoned after the failure of the "fashion show" bombing, or if there was a new assassination plan in the works.

In the meantime, Mutti and Papa had removed the Hoffmanns from the resistance for their own safety. Last year, Max would have been fine with going into hiding, keeping out of sight until the end of the war. But he was no longer the same boy he had been in 1943. Meeting Frau Becker and her comrades had awakened something within him. He didn't know what to call this awakening, but a man like Stauffenberg seemed to be a living example of it.

The willingness to do what was right without fear or hesitation.

To act in opposition to everything the Nazis stood for.

Max couldn't imagine a man like that with a noose around his neck.

"He's still alive," Max said. "The Nazis will never get him."

Gerta laughed bitterly. "He's human, Maxi. He can die like everybody else."

Max shook his head. "He's not like everybody else."

FOUR

JUNE 7, 1944
D-DAY PLUS ONE

The view from the Berghof, Hitler's residence in the Bavarian Alps, was spectacular. From the cliffside perch of the compound, a dense forest cascaded down to unfurl in patches through the rolling hills of the valley below. Where the trees parted, bits of the low foliage that carpeted the valley could be seen, lush and bright in the summer sun. For Claus von Stauffenberg, it brought to mind his childhood on the family estate in Lautlingen, four hundred kilometers west of the Berghof. Long afternoons shouting poetry at his brother Berthold as the two of them clambered over the rocky outcrops high above the clover fields, gazing out across an evergreen wood that hid endless mysteries.

Stauffenberg could almost hear Berthold shouting back, quoting their hero, the poet Stefan George: "The summer field is parched with evil fire . . ."

Evil fire.

The phrase lodged itself in Stauffenberg's unquiet mind. And no wonder, he thought as he stepped into the stifling conference room in the bowels of the Berghof. Here, at the table, were the men responsible for bringing evil fire down upon the summer fields of Europe. And now, with the Allies finally landed in France, they would begin to reap what they had sown.

But not soon enough, he reflected, sweeping his eyes along the faces of the Nazi high command as the men pored over detailed situation maps.

There was Albert Speer, Hitler's chief architect and Reich Minister of Armaments and War Production. With his probing countenance and a mind both focused and wide-ranging, Speer was the only man in the room who Stauffenberg was not immediately revolted by. Instead, he inspired within Stauffenberg a sad kind of wonder that such a brilliant architect and clear thinker should have devoted himself to the cause of a vicious, petty madman.

Next to Speer sat Field Marshal Keitel, Hitler's most dependable toady in the military. Nervous and grasping, Keitel was forever concerned with falling out of favor with Hitler. Stauffenberg took some small measure of satisfaction in the fact that the man was not seated next to Hitler, which was bound to make Keitel worried that his position among these men was far from secure.

After Keitel came Heinrich Himmler, the man responsible for the rise of the SS. Besides Hitler himself, Stauffenberg thought, there was no one more deserving of being hanged for crimes against humanity. Builder of death camps and organizer of mass exterminations, Himmler was a bland, bespectacled functionary who, with the stroke of a pen, authorized horrors on an incomprehensible scale.

But then, of course, there was the pasty Hermann Göring, Reich Minister of Aviation and Hitler's second-in-command, whose smug, childish grin was always plastered to his face—along with caked-on makeup that seemed to ooze in the humid air of the conference room. Stauffenberg could barely comprehend such a creature, even when Göring was standing right in front of him.

Were these men supposed to represent the ideal of the pure Aryan race, who would lead Germany's glorious thousand-year Reich? All Stauffenberg saw was a room full of scheming, sweating psychopaths.

He wished that his briefcase contained a bomb instead of papers. For the past few weeks, there had been no question in his mind that he would have to be the one to carry out the assassination of Adolf Hitler. There had been too many failures already, too many false starts and near misses, and the urgency was growing. Now, as he stepped toward the round table to meet the Führer himself, he was certain that he could do it without hesitation.

He would do it for what remained of Europe, and for the entire world. There were countless prisoners in the camps and soldiers on the front lines who could still be saved, if the Nazi high command was eliminated and Operation Valkyrie set into motion.

Stauffenberg presented his left hand, with its three remaining fingers. As Hitler grasped it in his own two hands, Stauffenberg noted a slight tremor in the Führer's grip. He also noted the way Hitler was forced to look up at him—Stauffenberg was considerably taller than the Nazi leader. He was surprised to find that Hitler's famously hypnotic gaze was a veiled shadow of its former self. Under Stauffenberg's cool appraisal, the Führer actually flicked his eyes away.

Careful, Claus, he admonished himself. Hitler was already paranoid—intimidating him or making him suspicious would only work against the Valkyrie plotters. Stauffenberg gave a deferential bow.

"My Führer," he said, brusque yet respectful, as befitting a man of Stauffenberg's impeccable reputation.

"Colonel," Hitler said, "how wonderful to finally meet you."

Hitler released Stauffenberg's hand, regarded him for a moment longer, then paced back around to the other side of the table. Stauffenberg felt the eyes of the other Nazi leaders on him, weighing the interaction for meaning, testing the air for subtle shifts in power. The atmosphere sapped his energy. This conference room was a stale, paralyzing place. He had not been here for very long—a minute or two—yet already he felt exhausted by the company of these men. News of the Allied invasion had them all subdued, that was to be expected— but there was something else, too. A seeping rot, a poison haze, a miasma that soured the air around them.

Well, no matter. This meeting had already achieved its goal, assuring Stauffenberg that his reputation among the high command was such that he could get himself invited to the Berghof, where he could move freely around Hitler himself.

He would not have to endure the company of these men much longer. Nor would the rest of the world. Soon, very soon, Claus von Stauffenberg would cleanse Germany of evil with a fire of his own.

FIVE

Operation *Valkyrie*, Max thought, remembering the name that Stauffenberg had given the plot to kill Hitler and remove the Nazis from power.

He sketched a curved line across the parchment paper balanced on the slab of wood in his lap. *Valkyrie.* The name conjured up a mighty winged creature, and Max penciled in rows of long feathers. The communist underground had dropped off pencils, charcoal, and a motley stack of paper, from newsprint to the heavy brown stuff that butchers used to wrap meat. (Max supposed that there wasn't much use for butcher paper when meat was scarce.) He found that he could easily lose himself in drawing. It proved to be a better way to pass the time than reading French theater programs over and over again.

Low voices from the radio drifted up the stairs. It was the third day after the D-Day landings, and Mutti, Papa, and Gerta were glued to the speaker. There had been talk of a

German secret weapon—some kind of land-based torpedo—that would push the Allies back into the sea. Max thought it was all a bluff, but secret weapon or no, the fighting was fierce and the Allies' progress slow. At this rate, inching across western France, it would take them until 1950 to reach Paris—forget about Berlin.

Max pressed the pencil harder into the page, darkening the line of the Valkyrie's steel helmet. He tried to imagine being stuck in this safe house for years and years, emerging into the sunlight as an old man with a long white beard.

Poor Kat, he thought. She was completely cut off from any news. Her mother could have been killed a month ago, and she would never know.

She hadn't said a word at last night's dinner—thin root-vegetable stew and some kind of mushy grain—and Max hadn't seen her since.

He set the drawing down and went to his window. Outside, it was another bright, sunny day. Their little side street at the northern edge of Prenzlauer Berg had been untouched by RAF bombs, and he stared at the plain, neatly kept row houses across the street, wondering if anybody else felt as cooped up as he did. He let the curtain fall back into place and counted his paces to the opposite wall—one, two, three, four.

He closed his eyes.

Valkyrie meant action. *Valkyrie* meant taking responsibility. *Valkyrie* meant changing things for the better.

Max thought of Kat Vogel, just across the hall, lying in bed in the middle of the day, staring up at the ceiling or sliding into fitful sleep.

Claus von Stauffenberg wouldn't just sit around and let her suffer in silence.

While Max thought this over, he heard his sister padding lightly up the stairs. He leaned out of his bedroom door and beckoned for her to come in.

"I think I know how to make Kat feel better," he whispered.

Gerta raised an eyebrow. "Max, no offense, but you might not be the best person for the job."

"We're all going crazy, cooped up in here." He sniffed the air. "It's not healthy."

"Better than a cell underneath Gestapo headquarters."

"I get why Mutti and Papa had to bring us here, Gerta," Max said. "I know we can't just live in our old house and act like nothing happened. But I think we should be able to take Kat out for some fresh air as long as we're careful, don't you?"

Gerta frowned. "Mutti and Papa will never let us go outside."

"I bet we can convince them if we work as a team. We've done it before."

"No." Gerta shook her head. Max recognized the sudden faraway look in her eyes: She was coming up with a scheme. "No, they'll never allow it . . . but I do think you're right.

Going outside is exactly what Kat needs. I think it's what I need, too." Her eyes went to Max's half-finished Valkyrie drawing. "And definitely what *you* need."

Max knew where this was going. "Gerta . . ."

She lowered her voice to the faintest whisper. Max leaned in close.

"Here's what we do," she said. "We wait till Mutti and Papa are sleeping, then wait another half hour to be sure. Then we go out the back door, into the yard, where the communists drop off our food. It's all overgrown. The weeds will hide us from any neighbors who might still be awake. As long as we wear dark clothes, we should be fine. The city's still blacked out at night."

Max recalled the night they'd spent in the public shelter, and his guts churned as the old woman's dead eye floated up from the place he'd buried it in the back of his mind.

"Every time we sneak out something bad happens," he said.

"Which is why nothing bad will happen this time," she said. "The universe owes us a favor."

"The universe isn't fair," he muttered.

Gerta hopped off the bed. "See you at midnight. Don't make me wake you up."

SIX

The back door to the safe house was stuck. Max turned the knob, pressed his shoulder against the door, and leaned forward with all his weight. It didn't budge. He glanced behind him at the shadowy figures of Gerta and Kat. The three of them were squeezed into the narrow passage behind the kitchen, a haven for muddy shoes and overcoats in happier times.

"It won't open," Max whispered. His voice sounded like a scream in the silence of the house after midnight. Even Papa's snoring had ceased—these days, it came in waves instead of being a steady presence throughout the night. Max thought that Papa must be tossing and turning, darting in and out of uneasy dreams. Being cooped up all day was not a recipe for a good night's rest.

"Let me," Kat said, stepping forward and nudging Max out of the way. She reached up and slid aside a metal latch that had been barring the door shut.

"I was just about to do that," Max said.

Kat turned the knob and opened the door slowly and carefully. Gerta and Kat stepped out into the dark backyard. Max followed, easing the door shut behind him, giving the knob a turn to make sure it was unlocked so they could sneak back in later.

They stood close together while their eyes adjusted. After a moment, an eerie night-garden took shape in the pale light of a sliver of moon, looming stalks of untended weeds as high as their heads and coils of brambles at their feet. Max breathed deeply. After so long inside the safe house, even the air of wartime Berlin tasted fresh and clean.

The weeds waved languidly in a light breeze. He listened to his sister and Kat take deep breaths of their own and felt a mild contentment settle over him. They were outside! He felt like he had been set free from the thoughts that spiraled endlessly through his head. How easy it was to get wrapped up in your own world when you were staring at the same walls all day long! They hadn't taken three steps from the door and already he felt sprung from his cage.

He wondered: Was this heady taste of freedom, of *action*, how Stauffenberg felt all the time?

"Come on," Kat said. She was whispering, but there was a spark of life in her voice—an eagerness he hadn't heard from her in several days. Max and Gerta let Kat lead them to the back fence, where another latch opened the gate out into the packed-earth alley behind the house. For Max, it recalled their flight from the Dahlem villa—a dim dream version of the February morning when they left their old lives behind. Some unexplainable sensation made him shiver. He saw his life in ever-narrowing circles, repeating variations, a symphony of hours, days, weeks . . .

A small change in the darkness made his heart leap. A window in an upper room of a neighboring flat was suddenly outlined in a blue-tinted glow. The outline became a wedge of light as a shadowed figure moved a curtain aside.

Max froze. Gerta and Kat moved on down the alley. He didn't dare call to them. They were all three dressed in black, yet Max felt completely exposed, as if the hidden eyes of the neighbor at the window were locked on his own.

Calm down. He cycled through his breathing exercise. It had been so long since he'd been sneaking around outside, he was out of practice. His brain could not separate danger from the normal goings-on in a quiet district like Prenzlauer Berg.

It's just somebody who can't sleep, he told himself, and hurried to catch up with Kat and Gerta.

The alley dumped them out onto a nondescript street crowded on both sides by modest row houses. Phosphorescent paint marked the sidewalk in neat stripes. To the east was the market, a long, low-slung building that took up nearly an entire city block. To the west was the community garden, a patch of pure, pitch-black emptiness. There was nobody out on the street.

Kat turned left, toward the darkness of the garden.

Leading the way, Kat moved with purpose, as if she had an urgent errand to run. When Max had come up with this plan of "getting some air," he hadn't given a moment's thought to where they would go once they were outside. Now he thought they should circle the block and go home before Mutti and Papa noticed they were gone. Or before something terrible happened.

He flashed to the ruined shelter, the cries of the lost and the injured, the unblinking eye . . .

"I think we should turn back," he said.

"I need trees," Kat said, picking up the pace.

"What?"

"Kat needs trees," Gerta said.

Max glanced over his shoulder, reassuring himself that the street was empty, then followed the girls up the sidewalk. Ahead, the blankness of the garden loomed, cut from the fabric of the night.

Kat broke into a jog and disappeared. Her shoes clip-clopped on the cobblestones.

Gerta ran to catch up, leaving Max alone in the dark. He hurried after the girls and joined them at the edge of the garden, where Kat was in some kind of strange thrall to a venerable old oak tree. She ran her hand along the grooves in the bark.

"My mother used to say that she could hear the trees breathe when she was a little girl," Kat said, putting her ear up to the trunk.

"I don't think that's possible," Max said. Gerta elbowed him in the gut.

"It feels like years since I've even *seen* a tree," Kat said.

Max and Gerta moved closer to the oak's thick trunk. Max closed his eyes and listened hard. After a moment, he could swear that he really did hear a faint rhythm—one, two, one, two, one, two . . .

"I think I hear it!" Gerta whispered.

Max began to worry as the rhythm grew louder. The noise was no gentle exhalation—it was something brutal and regimented, and it was getting closer.

"Get down," he said, pulling Gerta's sleeve. She dragged Kat down with them, and together they huddled in the deep shadows of the oak.

A moment later, the rhythm resolved into footsteps—heavy jackboots pounding the street in unison.

The telltale approach of Nazis.

An orange glow slid down the street, followed by its source: a flaming torch held aloft by a stocky, blond-haired boy in a light brown uniform with a hat that resembled the short-brimmed cap of a soldier.

He was flanked by a pair of unsmiling, heavyset teenagers holding torches of their own. Behind them marched a dozen more boys. They were all several years older than Max— sixteen or seventeen, he thought.

"Hitler Youth," Kat whispered in disgust.

Membership in the Hitler Youth had been compulsory since 1936. Karl and Ingrid Hoffmann had risked the suspicion of the authorities by not enrolling Max in the Hitler Youth or Gerta in the League of German Girls, but Karl's position as a surgeon working to save the city's bombing victims had given them a reprieve from some of the Nazis' restrictions. Still, Herr Siewert had reminded them over and over again that a boy like Max ought to be serving in the Nazi youth organization.

He remembered, with a rush of shame, how he had once wished to join one of the Hitler Youth soccer teams.

"What are they doing?" Gerta asked.

"It's some kind of patrol," Kat said.

Max watched the boys pass by in solemn procession. The torchlight flickered across their faces, giving their features an otherworldly cast. Papa said that boys from the Hitler Youth were already manning the heavy guns of Berlin's flak towers, and that when the Allies reached Berlin, Hitler would force the boys to fight in the streets. So many would die in a pointless, last-ditch defense of the city.

If only Hitler had been blown up back in February at the fashion show, Max thought bitterly. Perhaps then, instead of cowering in the dark and waiting for a bunch of grim-faced Nazi boys to pass by, Max would be sleeping peacefully in his bed in the villa in Dahlem, safe in the knowledge that the war was over.

Next to him, he heard Kat scrabbling in the dirt.

"What are you doing?"

"Watch this," she said. Max sensed a blur of motion.

Suddenly, the boy bringing up the rear of the Hitler Youth patrol spun on his heels with a yelp and swatted the empty air. Something clattered to the ground at his feet.

A rock.

Max sucked in his breath. Kat had just thrown a rock at the Hitler Youth!

The boy leading the patrol stopped and held up a hand. The others halted behind him. He walked back along the row, carrying his torch, until he reached the last boy—squat, pudgy, dark-haired. In the flickering light, Max could see the boy rubbing his shoulder, squinting uncertainly at his leader through thick spectacles.

"What is it?" the leader said.

"I—I don't know, Heinrich," the boy said. "Something hit me."

"What hit you?" Heinrich brought the torch closer to the boy's chubby face, and the boy winced at the heat of the flame. "Out with it, Gerhard."

Gerhard swallowed. "I guess it was nothing."

"Was it *something*, or was it *nothing*? Make up your mind. There's no place for wishy-washy thinking in the Midnight Hunters."

Midnight Hunters? Max thought. It seemed as though this boy, Heinrich, had formed his own special squad of Hitler

Youth. That explained the nighttime patrol. Max doubted a torchlit procession down the street in the middle of the night was an official Hitler Youth outing.

The boy next to Gerhard snickered. "Maybe a bird flew into your fat behind."

"There's no birds out this late," Gerhard said.

"A bat, then."

The other boys chimed in.

"A whole family of bats."

"A British bomber."

"The entire Luftwaffe."

"Shut up!" Heinrich said, and the chatter ceased.

He turned back to Gerhard. "Get hold of yourself, soldier."

Gerhard clicked his heels together miserably. "Yes, sir."

Heinrich glared at the boy for a moment longer, then stalked back up to the front of the procession and beckoned for them to follow. It wasn't until the patrol had turned a corner and moved out of sight that Max felt safe enough to stand up.

"Are you trying to get us killed?" he hissed at Kat. "We're supposed to be out getting some air, not throwing rocks at the Hitler Youth!"

"It was just a little pebble," Kat said, smirking. "Calm down."

"I am calm!"

Gerta laughed. "Sure, Maxi. Calm as a flak burst. Have you tried listening to the trees breathe? It's very relaxing."

Max knew his sister would take Kat's side. She was probably kicking herself for not thinking of throwing a rock first.

"It's not funny!" Max said. It had been his idea to take Kat outside the safe house, and he felt responsible for her safety. "We're outnumbered, and nobody knows we're out here. If those boys caught us—"

"I thought you were supposed to be some kind of fearless resistance fighter," Kat said, folding her arms.

"Leave him alone, Kat," Gerta said.

"No, seriously—isn't that the whole reason my father's dead," Kat said, "and my mother's in a camp?"

"*Shhhh!*" Gerta said.

"Don't tell me to *shhhh!*" Kat said. "I thought I was moving in with a family of fighters, but all I see is a bunch of people sitting around a smelly old house while the Hitler Youth walk up and down the streets like they own the city."

"We did our part," Max said.

"Well, good for you," Kat said. "Now I'm going to do mine."

Max sighed. "Okay, but . . . throwing rocks is stupid."

"I see," Kat said. "And what do you suggest?"

"We have to be smart," Gerta said. "We can't fight them physically. They'll kill us."

"We have to be like Albert," Max said.

Kat frowned. "Who's Albert?"

"A shadow," Max said.

SEVEN

On the way home Max felt light and free, propelled by the promise of action. Claus von Stauffenberg would approve. The tall officer would not let this gang of Hitler Youth—the Midnight Hunters—own the streets of his neighborhood.

Fighting them with fists and rocks would be suicide. But there were plenty of other ways to make their lives miserable.

His mind raced with thoughts of sabotage—laxatives in their food, itching powder in their shiny boots, all manner of vermin loosed upon their headquarters . . .

Tomorrow, they would begin to plan. Tomorrow, they would have a purpose.

Frau Becker might be dead, but the spirit of resistance lived on in them.

In the alley behind the safe house, he glanced up at the neighbor's window. The blue-tinted light had been turned off.

The house was dark. In a few hours, dawn would break over the city, and Max was looking forward to being fast asleep by then.

Gerta opened the gate in the back fence and held it ajar for Max and Kat to creep into the yard. She shut it behind her with a soft *click*.

Max was picking his way through the brambles when he felt a hand on his shoulder.

"Wait," Kat whispered. "I'm not ready to go inside yet. Just a few more minutes. Please."

That was fine with Max. It might be some time before they managed to sneak out again, and he intended to enjoy every last second in the open air.

They paused near the back door to the safe house. Gerta bent to pick at the weeds. Kat raised her eyes to the sliver of moon. Max lost himself in thoughts of the future. He had been mired in the past for so long, shuffling numbly through his days, that getting excited about *tomorrow* was jarring. Now that the Allies had landed, he could even glimpse the end of the war—distant, yes, but not out of reach. Then his life would be filled with the promise of endless tomorrows. As the years passed and he grew up, those months he spent pacing back and forth in the sweaty flat in Prenzlauer Berg would be nothing more than a half-remembered dream.

When the gate in the back fence swung open behind them, his first thought was that Gerta hadn't latched it properly.

Then the dark shape of a man entered the backyard and shut the gate behind him, as silently as Gerta had, and began to step lightly through the brambles. He was heading straight for them.

There was nowhere to go. They were trapped in the small, overgrown, fenced-in yard.

Max took a single step back toward the house. Dry leaves crunched beneath his shoe.

The intruder froze. He was barely visible in the moonlight, a silhouette outlined in the palest glow.

Then the moonlight glinted off something in his hand.

It was the long silver blade of a fearsome knife.

The Gestapo had found them at last. There would be a green minna parked out front. More agents surrounding the house. In a matter of seconds they would kick in the door and rush into the flat, dragging Mutti and Papa from their bed.

"Who are you?" the man demanded in a low but insistent whisper.

Max was flooded with relief at the sound of the familiar voice. "Papa!" he whispered in reply.

The blade vanished into the darkness. The man came forward. "Max!" Up close, Max could just barely make out his father's face. Papa was wearing a black fedora with the brim pulled low.

Papa carries a knife, Max thought. *A big one*. After all the family had been through with the Becker Circle, Max thought there were no more secrets between the Hoffmanns.

Of course, Max had just snuck out without telling anyone. And it looked like Papa had done the very same thing.

In Berlin, keeping secrets was a hard habit to break.

"Hi, Papa," Gerta said.

"Gerta," Papa whispered. "Kat. I see you're all in this together. Whatever *this* is. Come—let's talk inside."

EIGHT

Colonel Stauffenberg is alive," Papa said. "As far as we can tell, he wasn't betrayed. On the contrary, it appears that he will soon be promoted to chief of staff of the Reserve Army. Operation Valkyrie is still very much in motion."

They were huddled around the small kitchen table, four sets of eyes catching the light from the room's lone bulb.

Max elbowed Gerta. "Told you." He turned to Papa. "Is that who you were outside meeting with just now? Colonel Stauffenberg?"

He imagined the two men furtively ducking into an alley or striding past one another and exchanging a briefcase without slowing down.

Papa shook his head. "No, Maxi. It's far too dangerous for him to do that. We have reports that Hitler has grown so paranoid that he rarely leaves his residence at the Berghof. His suspicion knows no bounds, and we can't take unnecessary risks—not when Colonel Stauffenberg is so close to carrying out the assassination."

"Then—he's going to do it *himself*?" Gerta said.

"Yes," Papa said. "He has come to believe that it is too great a responsibility to entrust to anyone else."

Max's throat went dry. He thought again of the fashion show plot. The young lieutenant was going to strap himself with a bomb and explode it while he stood close to the Führer.

Killing Hitler was a suicide mission.

Stauffenberg would not live to see Valkyrie through. He would be killed along with Hitler, and leave the rest of the plot—neutralizing the SS, taking control of the government, making peace with the Allies—to his fellow conspirators.

"There has to be somebody else who can do it," Max said.

"Colonel Stauffenberg has access to Hitler's inner circle," Papa explained. "He's a man with an impeccable reputation, respected by the high command. There is no one else who can get close enough."

Max wondered if Stauffenberg had a family. Was it an agonizing decision for a man like that, to sacrifice his life? Or was he so bound by his duty to eliminate the Nazis' grip on Germany that he never doubted himself?

"How do you know all this?" Gerta said.

"You were meeting with Albert just now," Max guessed. "Or the princess."

"I'm afraid not," Papa said. "I suspect the princess has fled

Berlin. As for Albert, who knows? The man is an expert at not being seen. I know as much as you do of his whereabouts."

"So you were just enjoying the night air," Kat said, "like us."

No one spoke for a moment. Max half expected Papa to simply agree and move on, keeping the purpose of his late-night errand to himself.

"Not exactly," Papa said. He placed a small wooden box on the table, setting it down very gently. "I was meeting an old friend from the hospital." He lifted the lid of the box. "He gave me these."

Inside the box were six long glass vials shaped like miniature hourglasses. Max reached across the table to examine one of the curious items. Papa's hand darted out to grab his wrist.

"Careful! You don't want to touch them." He paused. "*I* don't want to touch them. They're filled with sulfuric acid."

Papa released his wrist. Max put his hands safely in his lap. "Oh," he said. "Right. Sulfuric acid."

No one spoke for a moment. The vials looked perfectly harmless, six little glass containers nestled snugly in the leather that lined the box. Each one was filled with clear liquid.

Papa was staring at them like he couldn't quite believe what he'd just brought into the house.

"Papa," Max said.

"Hmm?" Papa blinked and wiped his spectacles on his shirt.

"Why do you have six vials of sulfuric acid?"

"Ah," Papa said, replacing his spectacles. Max studied his father's face. Months of idleness had infected Karl Hoffmann with an absentmindedness he'd never possessed while he was working long days and nights at the hospital. "They will act as timers."

"Like . . . clocks?" Kat said. She began tapping out a soft waltz on her kneecaps.

"Not exactly." Papa took off his hat, set it on the table, and rubbed his temples. "I'm sorry. It's been a very long night." He looked at Max, Gerta, and Kat in turn. "Timers for the fuses. They'll arm the bombs that Colonel Stauffenberg uses to blow up Adolf Hitler." He pointed at the skinny, tapered midsection of one of the vials. "Once the glass is broken, here, the acid will begin to eat through the detonation wire. When it severs the wire completely . . . *kaboom*. No more Führer."

And no more Stauffenberg, Max thought.

"How long does it take to blow up, after the glass is broken?" Gerta asked.

"They tell me it takes ten minutes," Papa said. "Though I understand it is far from precise."

"So he could plant the bomb and still have time to get away," Max said.

"Yes," Papa said. "But I believe that Colonel Stauffenberg will do whatever it takes to ensure that the assassination succeeds. And if that forces him to hold the bomb until the very last second, then that is what he will do."

"When's he going to do it?" Max said.

"The bombs will be ready by the end of the week. Then it will depend on when the colonel gets invited to a conference with the Führer. He has no control over these invitations, so he must be ready to act at a moment's notice. I doubt we will know the day in advance."

Max tried to imagine what it would be like to wait around for the moment when you were summoned to meet with Adolf Hitler, knowing that you would be carrying a hidden bomb.

Max's chest felt tight. The kitchen was very small, the walls too close together and creeping closer. The lamp receded to a distant pinprick of blue light. Papa was suddenly very far away.

His thoughts veered abruptly to Uncle Friedrich, vaporized by a Soviet rocket attack thousands of kilometers from home.

The tiny speck of lamplight burned brighter, bursting into a corona of blue flame—an explosion from a briefcase bomb, a howling *Katyusha* rocket, a four-thousand-pounder dropped from the belly of an Avro Lancaster . . .

"Max." The voice was far away. Fire swirled in the oceanic depths of an unblinking eye—the eye of an old woman buried in the ruins of a bomb shelter, the eye of Claus von Stauffenberg, the eye of the world . . .

"*Max.*" Louder now. Papa's hand shook his shoulder. "*Breathe, Max.*"

After a few measured breaths, the flames died away and the shape of the kitchen emerged from Max's vision. His heart was pounding. Gerta and Kat were watching him, their eyes wide with alarm.

"That's it," Papa said. "You're safe here."

Max wiped sweat from his brow. "I'm sorry, everybody."

"It's okay," Gerta said.

"I think it's time we all got some sleep," Papa said. "We can talk more in the morning."

As he was trudging upstairs to his room, Max realized that nobody had thought to ask Papa about the knife.

NINE

The next week did nothing to reassure Kat that the Allies would reach Berlin anytime soon. The news from the BBC was all about how the Allies were "linking up the beaches." On D-Day, Max had imagined troops storming a single beach stretching endlessly in both directions along the French coast. But the invasion force had actually landed on five distinct beaches, code-named Utah, Omaha, Gold, Juno, and Sword. Once the beachheads were secured, and German troops painstakingly dislodged from their Atlantic Wall, the Allies' work had barely begun.

Meanwhile, the Germans were throwing their elite SS Panzer divisions into the fray, engaging the Allies in fierce battles for the inland French towns of Caen and Bayeux.

The Normandy front seemed poised to descend into a vicious deadlock. British Cromwell tanks were no match for German Tigers. On the other hand, Allied air power was virtually unchallenged.

Paratroopers, bombs, and artillery shells rained down on western France.

Prisoners on both sides were executed.

French civilians died.

German radio gleefully reported atrocities committed by the bloodthirsty Allies. RAF bombing attacks flattened French villages occupied by Germans. The towns of Villers-Bocage and Tilly-sur-Seulles were practically vaporized.

Allied radio urged the French resistance to rise up.

Max wondered what the Allies knew of the resistance in Berlin. As he pondered this, he realized that his own view of the resistance was limited to the Becker Circle and Stauffenberg's plot.

He thought of Papa and his vials of acid, which he had passed along to the communist underground, who would in turn pass them along to someone else in the resistance. Like this, the deadly fuses would make their way to Stauffenberg— the key ingredient for his briefcase bomb.

Max wished there was an exact date assigned to the assassination. Then he could fix the day in his mind instead of waking up in the middle of the night wondering if Stauffenberg was boarding a plane to the Berghof at that very moment.

While they waited, Max, Gerta, and Kat began to form their plan to take on the Hitler Youth of Prenzlauer Berg.

"We need a name," Max said one afternoon, lounging in his room. It was the middle of June. The radio was on downstairs.

There had been a new development from the Germans—it turned out that there actually *was* a secret "vengeance weapon," the V-1 "buzz bomb," a sort of robotic rocket that could be launched from sites in France to strike at the heart of London. The first V-1s had just exploded in the British capital.

He knew that Mutti and Papa only listened to the radio in hopes of hearing the breaking news that Hitler had been killed. It could happen anytime—tomorrow, next week, next month.

"Who's *we*?" Kat said. She was sitting cross-legged on the floor, tapping out a beat on the pile of theater programs. Dust swirled up from the pages.

"He means a code name for our mission," Gerta said. "He *loves* code names."

"Not for the mission," Max said, "for our group. If they're the Midnight Hunters, then we should be something better."

"Maybe we should actually *do* something before we give ourselves a name," Kat said. They had not been back outside since the night they encountered the Hitler Youth. Papa seemed to accept that they were simply getting some air, and Max and Gerta didn't want to push their luck by sneaking out again too soon.

Max felt bad about keeping this new secret from Mutti and Papa—especially after Papa had been so honest with them about Stauffenberg's plan—but in the end, he thought it was best not to worry them.

"How about *the Thorns*?" Max said. "Because we're going to be a thorn in the side of the Hitler Youth."

Gerta glanced at the faded rosebushes on the peeling wallpaper in Max's room. "Very creative."

"It's too bad *Valkyrie* is taken," Kat said. "That's a good name."

"Maybe a different winged creature," Gerta suggested.

"*The Dragons!*" Max said.

"Better," Kat said.

"But not quite right," Gerta said. "It's missing something."

"*The Red Dragons*," Max suggested.

Gerta made a face. "Why red?"

"I don't know," Max said. "Blood? Fire?"

Kat groaned in frustration. "So far we've thrown one pebble. That hardly sounds like the activities of red dragons."

"You're right," Max said. "Maybe after we do something, the name will just fall into place."

Kat's tapping ceased. "Tonight?" she said eagerly.

"Tonight," Gerta agreed.

"I was thinking," Kat said, "we should follow the Midnight Hunters. Find out if they have a headquarters, or at least some kind of meeting place."

"*The Young Valkyries*," Max said.

"Max," Gerta said.

"Stop," Kat said.

TEN

The group with no name made three more nighttime forays into the streets of Prenzlauer Berg before they saw the Midnight Hunters again.

It was the first week of July. In France, the battle for the city of Caen raged. In Berlin, the air was thick with the promise of a midsummer storm. Max, Gerta, and Kat were hiding beneath one of the oak trees at the edge of the community garden.

Max's stomach rumbled. The communist underground's delivery had been particularly scanty this week, and supper for the past two nights had consisted of thin, watery broth that tasted like spoiled fish and bread so crumbly they might as well have eaten the dust from the cellar steps.

He missed the days when Mutti could go out into the backyard and pick some carrots and tomatoes from the villa's kitchen garden.

"This is pointless," Gerta said. "They're not coming."

"It feels like we dreamed them up," Max said. He plucked a

long blade of grass and wondered what it would taste like. How bad could it be? Certainly not worse than ersatz bread.

"Don't get discouraged," Kat said. "Boys like that love to march around. We'll see them again eventually."

Max nibbled on the blade of grass. It tasted like dirt with a slightly bitter tang. He decided he could easily eat grass if he had no other choice.

Gerta nudged him. "What are you doing?"

"Tasting a piece of grass."

"Okay. I think it's officially time for us to go."

"*Shhh!*" Kat said. "Listen."

Max's heart quickened: There it was! The one-two, one-two of jackboots on cobblestones. They flattened themselves out beneath the tree, just as the torchlight began to flicker down the damp sheen of the pavement. A moment later, the patrol marched into view. There was Heinrich in the lead, carrying the biggest, brightest torch. This time, the two heavyset boys that had flanked him like bodyguards were half dragging, half carrying a boy with a black hood pulled down over his head. His hands were bound with rope.

In front of the oak trees, Heinrich held up a hand to call for a halt. If Max were to stand up and start walking, he could reach the Hitler Youth leader in less than ten paces.

Heinrich turned to address his patrol.

"We have taken a sacred oath to defend the Fatherland," he announced, his voice echoing down the silent street. Prenzlauer

Berg was a district where everybody minded their own business, and Max knew that even if some of the locals disapproved of the Hitler Youth marching around and making noise in the middle of the night, they would never confront the boys. The Hitler Youth was an extension of the Nazi Party in every way.

"Just because we're not off fighting the Tommies in the west or the Russian dogs in the east," Heinrich continued, "doesn't mean that we're not surrounded by enemies *at all times*." He took a moment to survey his boys. "Berlin is a festering wound. The capital of the Reich is infected! Just last week, the Gestapo rooted a hundred filthy Jews out of the Weissensee Cemetery." He paused. "Hiding in a *cemetery*! Would any of you boys skulk in the shadows of the graves of your ancestors to save your own skins?"

"No, sir!" came the reply.

"They were eating *rats*. The same rats that nibbled on the flesh of the dead." He shook his head in disgust. "That is the mind-set of the Jew. He does not care how much disease and misery he spreads as long as his kind survives. But do not be fooled! For every Jew that cowers in our attics and our cemeteries and our tunnels, there is another Jew—or communist, or intellectual, or"—Heinrich made it seem like he could barely choke out the word—"homosexual"—the boys snickered—"that is working against us! Putting all his cunning and all his wickedness toward tearing down everything our Führer has built!

Making bombs. Poisoning food. Shooting Party members *in the streets*. I ask you: Can we afford to relax our vigilance?"

"No, sir!" The cry came in unison.

Heinrich stalked over to the boy in the hood. The captive must have sensed the heat of the torch flame, because he started whimpering.

"If one of us is weak, we are all weak. Can we afford to *be weak?*" he screamed at the hooded boy.

"No, sir!"

Heinrich lifted his torch and gestured toward the darkness of the garden. Max's body was a coiled spring. He tried to make himself completely flat.

"Now show him what strength is. Make him understand."

The two heavyset boys dragged the hooded boy through the oak trees at the edge of the park. Max fought the urge to close his eyes, as if that would make it all go away. The rest of the Midnight Hunters trooped behind the captive, chattering excitedly as they moved through the darkness no more than five paces from where Max, Kat, and Gerta hid. Heinrich and his torch brought up the rear. The light faded as they made their way into the center of the garden, where anemic tomato plants dangled from posts like dead men on barbed wire.

Carefully, Max, Gerta, and Kat turned around, keeping themselves as low to the ground as they could. They had an unobstructed view of the proceedings. Heinrich jammed his torch down into the soil.

"Hold him steady!" he commanded. The hooded boy was suspended with his arms across the bigger boys' shoulders. His toes barely touched the ground.

Heinrich took a step toward the captive and in one fluid motion buried his fist in the boy's stomach. Max heard the breath whoosh from the boy's mouth. His body tried to scrunch into itself, but the bigger boys held him fast. All he could do was bring his knees up weakly as he gasped for air.

"We have to do something," Kat whispered.

"There's too many of them," Gerta said. "Be still."

Max thought of Papa's knife. If he had the weapon with him now, that might give them a fighting chance. The element of surprise was on their side—maybe the sight of a dark figure rushing from the trees, torchlight glinting off his blade, would send the Midnight Hunters scattering into the night.

He dismissed that notion as quickly as it came. He had never held a knife for a purpose other than buttering bread or cutting a piece of schnitzel. And Papa's knife was far bigger than the dull silverware in the kitchen—it was practically a sword! He would probably just hurt himself. Besides, there were still too many Midnight Hunters for one boy with a blade to take on.

Still, the thought was lodged in his mind and would not let go. *Papa has a knife.*

"Put down the rock, Kat," Gerta hissed.

Max braced himself. If Kat launched a rock into the boys' midst, they would have to take off running and hope they could slip into the darkness of Prenzlauer Berg before the Midnight Hunters made it out of the garden.

"We'll get them," Gerta insisted, "just not like this."

"Who's next?" Heinrich called out.

A lanky boy with a gaunt, small-featured face stood before the captive. With a quick stutter-step approach, he delivered another blow to the boy's stomach. The boy squirmed and gasped for air.

"What's that?" Heinrich said, cupping a hand around his ear and leaning close to the struggling boy. "I can't hear you."

One of the heavyset boys cleared his throat.

"What is it?" Heinrich said.

"He's soiled himself, sir."

Heinrich glanced down at the captive's legs. His face was pinched, his mouth a thin line.

"Let him go," he said.

The heavyset boy frowned. "Sir?"

"Drop him," Heinrich said.

The boys stepped aside and the captive crumpled to the ground, curling up into a ball.

"Hopeless," Heinrich said, leaning down to address the boy, who was still wearing the black hood. "I wouldn't be surprised to find Gypsy blood in your veins."

Heinrich delivered a vicious kick to the boy's midsection, then turned and led his squad from the garden without another word.

Max tensed as the Hitler Youth once again passed close to his hiding spot. The boys were subdued. A few looked back over their shoulders into the darkness of the garden.

One boy spoke up. "Are we just leaving him there, sir?"

"Let him find his own way home," Heinrich said, leading the procession down the street.

When they were out of sight, Max, Gerta, and Kat stood up. Gerta clicked on a small electric torch and swept the beam across the tomato plants.

The boy looked like a pile of rags in the dirt. They hurried over to him. Max wrinkled his nose at the sharp smell of urine. He reached down and pulled off the boy's hood.

The boy yelped in fright and tried to cover his face with his hands.

"We're not going to hurt you," Kat said.

Slowly, he lowered his hands. The torchlight paused on his face.

It was Gerhard, the Hitler Youth boy whom Kat had pelted with a rock!

ELEVEN

You!" Kat hissed.

The lenses in Gerhard's spectacles were webbed with tiny cracks. He squinted into the light.

"Who—who are you?" he sputtered.

"None of your business," Gerta said.

"Come on," Kat said, "let's get out of here."

"Wait," Max said. Maybe they didn't have to risk following the Midnight Hunters to their headquarters after all. "Why did they do this to you?" he asked, trying to sound as friendly and harmless as possible.

Gerhard sat up and started to cough. Gerta kept the light trained on his face so he couldn't see them clearly in the glare.

"We're supposed to be able to fight," he said. He slipped a finger under a cracked lens and rubbed his eye. "I'm not good at stuff like that."

"It's okay," Max said.

"The Midnight Hunters are only supposed to be the toughest boys."

Kat scoffed. "Why'd they let you in then?"

"Heinrich's dad and my dad are old friends. They're both Obersturmführers in the SS. I think his dad made him invite me." Gerhard's lip trembled. "I didn't want to do it in the first place. I hate it." He wiped his nose on the sleeve of his dirty brown uniform. "We just march around, and sometimes the SS tells us where people are hiding, and we . . . we . . ." Gerhard's body began to heave as he sobbed.

"Listen," Max said. He put a hand on Gerhard's shoulder. "We're not like Heinrich. We're not going to hurt you." He glanced at Kat and Gerta and shrugged. "We're your friends."

They waited for Gerhard to pull himself together. After a while, he stopped crying, and something besides misery flashed across his face. Suspicion? Max wondered.

"Who are you?" he asked again.

"The Red Dragons," Kat said. Max looked at her in astonishment. Now it was Kat's turn to shrug.

Gerhard looked puzzled. "Red Dragons?"

"Listen," Max said, "is there a place the Midnight Hunters meet up? Like a clubhouse or something?"

Gerhard sniffled and nodded. "The hunting lodge."

Max frowned. He flashed to the packet of maps the Becker Circle had pored over in Frau Becker's sumptuous sitting room. Wolf's Lair, Eagle's Nest, Führerbunker. "Is the hunting lodge out in the woods somewhere?" he prodded Gerhard. "Outside of the city?"

Gerhard shook his head. "The 'hunting lodge' is what Heinrich calls it. It's really just a building on Stargarder Strasse, near the Gethsemane Church."

Max had seen the church before—a stately redbrick structure with a tall pointy steeple and a statue of some saint or another out front, raising a hand in blessing. It was on the corner of a quiet tree-lined street of spacious row houses with balcony windows.

"What's the building look like?" Gerta said.

Gerhard narrowed his eyes. Max didn't like the crafty look that was beginning to replace the despair on his face. "Why do you want to know?" He tried to move his head to see past the torch beam's glare. Gerta moved the light along with him. "What are you doing here, anyway?"

"We're your friends," Max said again.

"I don't know you." Gerhard tried to scramble to his feet. Kat grabbed his shoulder and shoved him back down.

"We're your friends *as long as you answer our questions*," she said, her voice low and mean.

Max shot her a look of annoyance. He thought he was on the right track with his gentle, coaxing approach. If they bullied Gerhard like Heinrich did, the boy was just going to shut down.

Besides, Gerhard might be a member of the Hitler Youth,

but Max actually felt a pang of sympathy for him. He was a victim of the stronger, more aggressive boys' whims.

Then he remembered how he'd tried to help Herr Siewert in the ruins of the shelter, and the Nazi *blockwart* had used his dying breath to wish Max and his family dead.

He reminded himself that the Hitler Youth were Nazis through and through. Gerhard's father was a high-ranking SS man.

He let Kat keep her hand clamped down on Gerhard's soft shoulder.

Gerhard swallowed. "I can't tell you," he said. "It's a secret place. Midnight Hunters only."

"Here's the thing, Gerhard," Max said. "We're going to find out one way or another. You can save us a little time by helping us out right now."

Gerhard opened his mouth. Then he thought the better of it. He rubbed a hand along his ribs and winced. "Heinrich will kill me," he said.

Kat laughed coldly. "Do you know what the Red Dragons do, Gerhard?"

The boy shook his head miserably. Max raised an eyebrow at Kat—he was also curious about what, exactly, the Red Dragons did.

"We hunt the hunters," Kat said.

"We can protect you from Heinrich," Gerta said.

At this, Gerhard laughed. "The three of you?" He closed his eyes. "You know what? It doesn't matter." Hysteria turned his voice loud and ragged. "Heinrich will kill me. He'll kill you, too. Then at least we'll be done with all this, right?" He cackled. "The hunting lodge is at eleven Stargader Strasse, next to the bakery."

Kat removed her hand from his shoulder. Gerhard pushed himself to his feet, breathing hard. For a moment, the torchlight slipped off his face, and Max was sure he got a good look at the "Red Dragons."

Then he turned and trudged off into the darkness without another word.

Gerta trained the light on the dirt where he'd fallen. "What's that?" she said. It looked like crumpled identification papers or ration cards.

Max picked up three small rectangles of stiff paper and smoothed them out in his hand. Gerta trained her light on the cards. Each one featured a portrait photograph of a man in military dress, with the swastika prominently displayed on his armband.

The first was a thickset man with a cleft chin perched on the turret of a Panzer tank. "Obergruppenführer Sepp Dietrich," Max read in the photograph's caption. He turned the card over. "From his roots as a humble, hard-working butcher, Dietrich distinguished himself on the front lines in the First World War. After the Armistice, he commanded the Führer's personal SS bodyguard—"

Kat ripped the cards from Max's hand. "Nazi war hero

trading cards," she said. "The Hitler Youth collect them." She tore Obergruppenführer Sepp Dietrich into little bits and let the pieces flutter to the ground. Then she did the same to the others.

"Let's go," she said. "We've got to plan our visit to eleven Stargader Strasse."

TWELVE

JULY 11, 1944

Claus von Stauffenberg's staff car turned onto the lane that sliced through the dense forest surrounding the Berghof. In the driver's seat, Lieutenant Werner von Haeften, Stauffenberg's aide-de-camp, gripped the steering wheel with his shoulders hunched and his mouth set in a grim line. His lips were bloodless, his face as ashen as the slightly overcast sky that unfurled above the Bavarian wilderness.

"Try to relax, Werner," Stauffenberg said. "It's only an assassination, after all."

Haeften's mouth twitched. His eyes flicked to the handsome brown leather briefcase Stauffenberg held in his lap. "I wish there was another way."

Stauffenberg gave an impatient huff. "Caen is in ruins. We hold out pointlessly, dividing our forces into smaller and smaller divisions to cover ground we can't possibly hold, while the Allies level cities to the ground and call it *liberation*. To say nothing of the Soviet front, which will be at the gates of

Warsaw before the summer is out. No, Werner, there has not been another way for quite some time. The generals, so far, have done nothing. It is time for the colonels to act."

"I mean, I wish there was someone else to deliver the . . . package. If we could only get Rommel to—"

"Rommel is a lost cause," Stauffenberg said. "He likes being a hero to the German people too much. If we succeed, then he will magically appear at the forefront of our conspiracy in a puff of smoke. Wait and see."

"And if we fail?"

Stauffenberg ran a finger along the brass buckle that latched the briefcase shut. *Where will this little piece of metal end up?* he wondered. Embedded in the Führer's forehead? Himmler's breastbone?

He shrugged. "Then he will condemn us, like all the others. Or Hitler, in his madness, will have him shot."

The lane brought them out of the shelter of the forest. The bald outcrop where Hitler's residence was perched came into view. Beyond it, the splendor of Bavaria unfolded in clover fields and rolling hills that galloped toward a low haze in the distance. Haeften downshifted and the staff car shuddered as he nosed down the steep approach to the Berghof.

Stauffenberg tightened his grip on the briefcase. It had been a simple matter to stay calm in the quiet of the ancient forest, but now they were pulling up to the garage behind the Berghof. He could already see the pair of SS bodyguards from the Reichssicherheitsdienst who would meet him as he stepped out of the car. They were fiercely loyal men who would not hesitate to shoot anyone they suspected threatened their Führer—even if that man was as well regarded as Claus von Stauffenberg.

Lightly, he ran a finger along the side pocket of the briefcase. Inside were the special pliers that would allow his three working fingers to break the vial of acid inside the fuse, arming the bomb that sat dormant inside the case.

"Get out of there as fast as you can," Haeften said.

"I do not plan to linger," Stauffenberg said. After he planted the bomb, Haeften would race him back to the airfield, where a plane was waiting to return him to Berlin to coordinate the Valkyrie takeover.

Eliminating Hitler, Himmler, and whomever else on the high command they should be lucky enough to kill was only the first step. For this reason, it had been decided that Stauffenberg's survival was essential. There was nobody else who could bring the many threads of the conspiracy together in the aftermath of the assassination.

The SS must be neutralized and the government turned over to army officers dedicated to making peace with the Allies.

Haeften brought the car to a halt in the shadow of the Berghof's rear wing. He got out, gave a German greeting to the SS men, walked briskly around the front of the car, and opened the door for Stauffenberg.

The colonel stepped out and gave a curt nod to the bodyguard who approached him. "Heil Hitler," he said with just a hint of dismissiveness. An aristocratic bearing came naturally to Stauffenberg, and he found it useful as he navigated the corridors of Nazi power.

"Colonel," the SS officer said, reaching for the briefcase. "Allow me."

Stauffenberg tucked the briefcase under his arm. "I can manage, thank you."

His self-sufficiency was not out of the ordinary. In North Africa, after the American P-40 had strafed the column of vehicles carrying him, resulting in the wounds that would take his hand, two of his fingers, and his eye, Stauffenberg had refused pain-killing drugs as the surgeons labored to save his life.

Now he could barely remember what he did with all ten fingers when he'd had them, anyway. What good was a pinkie?

He followed the SS officer into the residence. The hall was dimly lit, and the row of small windows did little more than drag the afternoon's gloom inside.

The briefcase seemed to grow heavier with every step. He wondered, not for the first time, if a time bomb was a coward's weapon. During this long, infernal summer of 1944, he had often dreamed of these horrid conferences, his dream self sitting at the long table and stewing in quiet rage, barely listening as lackeys like Field Marshal Keitel indulged the

Führer's mad whims, and the petty, childish fury that had led to the deaths of so many millions.

Forbidding the Sixth Army to surrender at Stalingrad, even after all hope was lost.

Sending V-1 rockets screaming into London and assuring the German public that the scattered attacks would bring the Allies to their knees.

These dreams always unfolded the same way: Stauffenberg jumped to his feet, drew a hidden pistol, and put two bullets into the Führer's brain at point-blank range.

These dreams always ended the same way, too: The SS bodyguard emptied his Luger into Stauffenberg's torso. At the moment of his death, his eyes would snap open in the dark and he would sit up, breathing so hard that his wife, Nina, would awaken from her own slumber to lay a comforting hand on him.

Nina . . .

The children . . .

"Sir?" The voice of the SS bodyguard shook him from his reverie. *Focus, Claus!* He must keep his wits about him.

"Yes?"

They turned down a narrow hallway lined with lurid paintings depicting events in Hitler's favorite opera: Wagner's *Ring Cycle.* There was Wotan, king of the gods, with his long white beard and wooden staff. The smell of savory vegetable stew drifted down the corridor. Hitler, Stauffenberg knew, was a vegetarian.

"I said I put in a request to be rotated to the Normandy front," the SS man said.

"Did you?" Stauffenberg asked dryly.

"I want to kill as many Tommies as I can. My sister died in Hamburg."

"I'm sorry," Stauffenberg said.

They passed a portrait of Wotan's daughter, Brünnhilde the Valkyrie, brandishing a silver sword.

Stauffenberg allowed himself a tiny smile. *Valkyrie, give me strength* . . .

"And the Americans and the Canadians," Stauffenberg said, "will you kill them, too?"

"All of them," the SS man said.

"I hope you get your chance," he said, thinking, *Very soon you will be reunited with your sister.*

Stauffenberg recalled the labyrinth of corridors from his last visit to the Berghof. One more left turn, and then he would inform the SS officer that he needed to visit the washroom before stepping into the briefing room for an audience with the Nazi high command. It would not do for an officer of his stature to arrive looking travel-weary and disheveled. In the privacy of the washroom stall, he would use his special set of pliers to crimp the fuse and clip the glass vial, setting the acid free to eat through the detonator. Then he would walk into the meeting, find a way to place the briefcase as close to the Führer and Himmler as possible, excuse himself to make an emergency call to Berlin, and hurry out of the Berghof and into Haeften's waiting car. God willing, they would be through the perimeter checkpoint before the bomb exploded.

He had to make sure his timing was perfect.

"I'm afraid I'm running a bit late," Stauffenberg said. "Tell me—has everyone arrived?"

"Everyone but Reichsführer Himmler," the SS man said.

Stauffenberg's heart quickened. He swallowed his surprise. "Oh? Airplane delay?"

"I only know what they tell me, which isn't much, but I believe he's held up indefinitely in Berlin."

They took a left. The washroom door was twenty paces away. It was now or never.

Stauffenberg cursed silently. If the Operation Valkyrie plotters had had half the luck of these damned Nazis, the war would have been over in 1943.

Ten paces.

He already knew that Hermann Göring wasn't in attendance. He could still assassinate the Führer himself, but he had been counting on, at the very least, taking out Hitler's second-in-command, Himmler.

To kill Hitler, but leave both Himmler *and* Göring alive?

No. It was not enough. It left too many powerful Nazis alive and in a position to quickly work against the army's takeover.

With a heavy heart, he let the SS bodyguard lead him past the washroom to the windowless chamber. As he opened the door, Adolf Hitler looked up from a huge map of the Normandy front. The Führer looked haggard and exhausted. When he stepped forward to greet Stauffenberg, he dragged his left leg.

Stauffenberg composed himself. He would have to sit calmly in a two-hour meeting in this stifling room with a dormant bomb at his feet.

He would have to give a presentation on the state of the Reserve Army, for which he had barely prepared.

All the while, poor Haeften would have to wait outside, wondering what had gone wrong.

His fellow plotters manning the phones back at the Reserve Army headquarters in the Bendlerblock would be waiting for word of the explosion. His friends and coconspirators General Beck in Berlin, Henning von Tresckow in Russia, and Karl Heinrich von Stülpnagel in Paris were all waiting to issue commands to neutralize the SS.

He thought of the brave resistance fighters holed up in safe houses in Berlin, wondering if all their efforts had been fruitless, waiting by the radio to hear news of the Führer's demise.

THIRTEEN

ax's hands were sticky with pokeweed berry juice. He sat on his bedroom floor alongside Gerta and Kat, mashing the bright red berries into a small bowl, mixing them up into a crimson slurry. A hardy plant, the pokeweed grew wild in the backyard, and though its berries were inedible—poisonous, Mutti warned—the Red Dragons had found a way to put them to use.

Kat was busy tearing a piece of butcher paper into small squares. On each square, Max had drawn a simple logo: a dragon with pointy teeth and majestic wings. Kat handed him one of the dragons. Max dipped a finger into the bowl and smeared some of the berry paste across the dragon's belly. He colored in the lines as best he could, then set the paper aside to dry and moved on to the next one.

The Nazi war hero trading cards had given Gerta the idea that the Red Dragons needed a calling card of their own. They wanted the Hitler Youth to believe that a well-organized resistance group was responsible for their troubles.

Troubles that were set to begin tonight.

"Remember Kristallnacht?" Kat said.

The night of the broken glass. Max had been six years old in November of 1938, as the Nazis and their sympathizers rampaged through the streets of Berlin, smashing the windows of Jewish-owned shops, vandalizing synagogues with sledgehammers, and murdering Jewish citizens while the police looked the other way.

At the time, the violence and the damage had seemed unreal to Max. He couldn't imagine the years of Nazi horrors to follow, full of devastation that would make broken glass and angry mobs seem almost quaint by comparison.

"Of course I do," he said, mashing red paste into the third dragon.

"Do you think Heinrich and his friends remember?" she asked slyly.

"Maybe they need a reminder," Gerta said.

As the girls plotted, Max finished smearing berry juice on the dragons. Then he went to the tiny washroom at the end of the hall to rinse the juice off his hands. As he did, Max paused, listening. Mutti and Papa were downstairs, flipping through newspapers and drinking tea.

His parents' bedroom was just across from the washroom. Max could see the door was ajar.

With a deep breath, he slipped inside. The curtains were

closed but it was a bright afternoon. There was enough light to make out the neatly made bed, the small bureau with its cracked mirror, and the night table cluttered with books and papers.

Max went to the bureau and opened the top drawer. There were two pairs of trousers and several shirts, perfectly folded. He closed the top drawer and opened the next one down. It was full of socks and undergarments. Gingerly, he poked around. Finding nothing, he closed that drawer and opened the bottom one. It was completely empty. He went to the nightstand and pulled open its single, small drawer.

There was the knife, sheathed in a sturdy black leather scabbard. Four metal rings protruded from the hilt, perfectly spaced to fit four fingers. *Knuckle duster*, Max thought—like the brass version that Lady Danger hid inside her purse on *Hornet and Wasp*. His father's knife was two weapons in one.

Carefully, he brushed a finger along the hilt. The metal was cool to the touch. The desire to heft it, test its weight and feel it in the palm of his hand, warred with the desire to close the drawer and leave the room.

He stood there for a moment, very quiet, listening. His parents were still downstairs. Gerta and Kat were talking quietly in his bedroom. Suddenly, without thinking, he found that he was lifting the knife out of the drawer. Keeping the blade sheathed, he slid his fingers through the rings and gripped the hilt. It was heavier than it looked. A little big for his hand, but not by much. Carefully, he began to pull the blade from its scabbard. Each side was honed to a fine edge.

The blade was halfway exposed when reality caught up with him and he thought: *I am holding a knife in Papa and Mutti's room.*

He set the knife gently into the drawer and slid it shut.

As he left the room, he vowed that he would never touch the knife again. He just wanted to know where Papa kept it. That was all.

FOURTEEN

Stargader Strasse was thoroughly blacked out. Not a single window leaked light, and the dabs of phosphorescent paint that marked the curb looked like they hadn't been refreshed in months.

Despite the faint breeze that stirred the air, it felt as if the day's trapped heat was radiating off the pavement. Max was struggling to keep up with the girls. He had done his share of sneaking around last winter, but Kat moved like a huntress on the prowl, melting into the darkness between the row houses and the spindly trees that lined the sidewalks. The spire of the Gethsemane Church loomed at the end of the block, a needle in the fabric of the night sky.

Suddenly, Kat stopped. "There's the bakery," she said, pointing to a shop in the center of the next block, where the taller row houses gave way to a low-slung commercial strip. The white paint on its sign advertising FRESH BAKED BREAD was just barely visible. "And there's number eleven, right next to it."

The Midnight Hunters' "hunting lodge" looked, to Max, like any other nondescript building on the block. One door, two ground-floor windows, two second-floor windows. Heinrich's father the SS Obersturmführer probably "appropriated" the building from a Jewish shop owner and gave it to his proud Nazi son.

"Okay," Max whispered. "Now we know where it is."

Tonight's mission was reconnaissance. They had planned to scope out the street, get a sense of the area, and figure out what kind of tools they would need to properly vandalize the Midnight Hunters' headquarters.

Broken glass was only going to be the beginning.

"I want to get closer," Kat said. Without waiting to see if Max and Gerta were following her, she hurried across the street toward number eleven.

Max grabbed his sister's sleeve. "I know where this is going."

"Come on," Gerta said. "Kat's just . . . being Kat."

Reluctantly, Max followed Gerta across the empty street. He could just barely make out Kat's dark figure stooping over to examine something on the ground in front of number eleven.

"Oh no," he muttered as they caught up with her. She was sifting through a pile of refuse that had collected against the curb. She straightened up triumphantly, holding a brick in her right hand.

"It must have come loose from the sidewalk," she whispered. Quickly, she reached into her pocket and pulled out one of the Red Dragon logo cards, along with a length of twine. With deft movements, she tied the card to the brick and finished with a little bow, like she was wrapping a gift.

"Kat," Max said, glancing up and down the street. "I thought we agreed that we were still in the planning stage."

"I am planning." She paused for a moment. "And now I'm doing."

With that, she launched the brick toward one of the ground-floor windows of eleven Stargader Strasse.

The noise was terrific—a burst of shattered glass, then a loud *thunk* as the brick struck something hard inside the hunting lodge. Almost immediately, lights blinked on behind closed curtains in row houses up and down the block.

The windows in the hunting lodge stayed dark. The boys were probably out on patrol.

"Time to go," Max said.

"One second." Gerta knelt down, dug through the refuse pile, and came up with a small stone. She reached back and rocketed the stone through the window, widening the hole made by the brick.

Max hesitated. Then he decided that he had to know what it felt like. He reached down and picked through the pile of food scraps and old newspapers until his hand closed around something smooth and hard.

"A beer stein," he said. The oversized mug was made of porcelain, cracked in two places, with a hinged copper lid. He let it fly. A sudden lightness came over him, a feeling of relief similar to when he came back to reality after one of his episodes. It might not be much—a single broken window—but for the first time since they'd gone into hiding, Max felt like a member of the Becker Circle once again.

This is for you, Frau Becker, he thought.

Already weakened by the brick and the stone, the entire window shattered and fell away, leaving a few pointy shards like jagged, irregular teeth around the frame.

Down the block, a door slammed, and the sound of hurried footsteps came pattering up the sidewalk.

Kat reached into her pocket and scattered a few more Red Dragon cards in front of the hunting lodge, then turned and sprinted across the street.

"You!" It was a man's voice, loud and commanding, coming out of the darkness. *"Stop!"*

Max and Gerta took off, heading east on Stargader Strasse, past the Gethsemane Church, where the old saint raised a stone hand to bless the night. Max felt like he could run for hours. Adrenaline surged through his veins. After a while, the footsteps faded behind him, then vanished altogether.

When they regrouped in the overgrown backyard of the safe house, their exhilaration made it nearly impossible to keep quiet.

That night, it was a long time before Max fell asleep. He thought of Heinrich and the rest of the boys returning from patrol to find the window of their hunting lodge smashed. He wished he could be a fly on the wall when the boys discovered the brick with the dragon attached.

The Red Dragons would have to be more careful and less impulsive now that the Midnight Hunters knew there was a resistance group operating in Prenzlauer Berg. Max and Gerta would have to rein in Kat before she got them killed. But tonight, he had to admit he was glad that she had simply decided to act. He would never forget what it felt like to send that beer stein crashing through the window.

In the moment before he finally drifted off, Max thought that Claus von Stauffenberg would approve.

FIFTEEN

Max found the bottle of absinthe in the very back of one of the kitchen cupboards, left by some previous resident—perhaps the collector of the theater programs. He knew his parents wouldn't miss the bottle. On the rare occasions Mutti and Papa touched alcohol, it was during Sunday dinner with Uncle Friedrich, or one of the holiday parties they threw for Papa's friends from the hospital.

No one was coming to dinner in the safe house, so the absinthe bottle just sat there gathering dust—until tonight.

It was two nights after the Red Dragons' glass-shattering raid on the hunting lodge. In France, the Americans were fighting to take the town of Saint-Lô and open up the breakout route all the way to Paris. In the east, the Soviets were pushing the Wehrmacht back toward Germany. The Red Army had already liberated Minsk, and just today, word came over the radio that Vilnius had fallen. Poland was now in striking distance. At this rate, Max thought, the Soviets would reach Berlin before the Allies could fight their way through France.

In Prenzlauer Berg, Max and Gerta were crouched in the grass at the edge of the garden. Max held the stoppered absinthe bottle close to his chest. Kat was at the other end of the garden, keeping an eye out for the Midnight Hunters.

"Does she ever talk about her father with you?" Max asked.

Gerta was silent for a moment. "A little. Why?"

"It's just strange, how we knew General Vogel from Frau Becker's sitting room, but he must have been so different around Kat."

"She loved him. A lot."

"Do you think we'll make it through the war? Our whole family, I mean?"

"Max." Gerta sounded weary. "Where is this coming from?"

"I don't know. It's just that one day Kat had both her parents, and the next day they were both gone."

"Listen to me." Gerta squeezed his hand. "Colonel Stauffenberg is going to kill Hitler any day now. And then everything's going to be different. You'll see."

They fell silent at a sudden rustling in the underbrush. A moment later, Kat slid into the grass beside them, breathing hard.

"They're two or three blocks away, on their usual route. I say go."

Max glanced up the street. He thought he could just make

out a pinprick of orange light floating in the darkness—
Heinrich's torch.

He took a deep breath and ran across the street, splashing
absinthe onto the pavement in a ragged line as he went. When
he reached the other side, he retraced his steps, applying a
second coat of the potent liquor. As the fumes rose up around
him, the aroma of sweet licorice seemed to wreath his head.

He paused briefly in the middle of the street to lay a Red
Dragon card down in front of the spilled liquid, then retreated
to the shelter of the trees at the edge of the garden.

"Your turn, fire girl," he said, setting the empty bottle down
in the dirt. Up the road, the torch was much closer, and he
could make out Heinrich's face along with hints of the brown-
uniformed boys at his back.

His sister held up the little book of matches that Mutti used
to light candles around the house. She flicked one of the
matches against the strike pad. Nothing happened.

"This one's a dud," she said, tossing the match aside and
taking another from the packet.

She struck the second match. Still nothing.

Max could hear the one-two, one-two of the Midnight
Hunters' boots. "Come on, Gerta."

"I'm trying," she hissed. "You two take off. I'll meet up with
you back at the house."

"Not in a million years," Kat said. "I want to see this."

Gerta struck a third match. This time, a tiny flame sprouted from its head. Carefully, she touched the flame to the edge of the spilled absinthe.

Bright green fire leaped from the pavement and snaked across the road, skating along the trail of spilled liquor. It was beautiful, Max thought. He wished he had the skill to pour the absinthe in the shape of a dragon, but it was too dark for that, and there wasn't much time. A wall of flame would have to do.

Of course, the "wall" was only about ankle-high, but absinthe was all they had. Next time they wanted to light a fire—a *real* dragon fire—they'd have to find some fuel.

As the patrol came into full view, the problem with their plan became apparent. In order to see Heinrich's reaction, they would have to remain huddled in the darkness at the edge of the garden—and the wall of flame pointed directly to their hiding spot. They might as well have painted a phosphorescent arrow—*Red Dragons this way!*

The Hitler Youth boys were close enough now for Max to see the puzzlement on Heinrich's face. There was something different about his uniform, too. A moment later Max realized what it was: the pistol holstered at his side.

"We have to go *now*," Max said as Heinrich called for a halt, then knelt down to examine the card lying in the road at the foot of the flames.

In the darkness, Max could just barely make out the curious look on Kat's face—a sort of openmouthed, trancelike eagerness.

"Kat!" Gerta hissed.

Too late. The rock pelted Heinrich in the belly. He doubled over. The two heavyset boys rushed to his side.

Max, Gerta, and Kat took off running, heading deeper into the community garden, churning up dry leaves and mulch. There was no time to be stealthy—they had to melt into the night, fast. They were moving through the tall grass just beyond the trees when Heinrich's enraged shouting began. *"Don't let them get away!"*

Max thought of the pistol on the Hitler Youth leader's hip. What did it feel like to get shot? Was it a fiery, piercing pain, or more like a paralyzing blow from a brickbat?

He did not intend to find out.

A quick glance over his shoulder revealed light from several torches bobbing madly as the boys dashed through the trees in pursuit.

"I thought we said no more rocks!" Gerta said.

"I couldn't help it, I swear," Kat said. "It was like something just took over my body."

Suddenly, a sharp blow to Max's side sent him sprawling in the dirt. *I've been shot!* he thought—but he hadn't heard the report of a pistol.

The air rushed from his lungs. The darkness seemed to slide around him, punctuated by star-bright flares. Stunned, he rolled over onto his back and tried to get his bearings. At the same time, he prodded his aching ribs.

He quickly determined that he wasn't bleeding. That was good. So what had taken him down? He sat up and found that he was surrounded by looming skeletal structures.

The tomato plants! He had sprinted full speed into one of the wooden cages that held the sad plants above the ground.

Ahead of him, Kat and Gerta had vanished into the night, heading toward the northern edge of the garden, which spilled out into the district of Pankow. They must not have realized that Max had gone down.

He glanced back toward the road. The wall of absinthe-flame was obscured by the trees, but the torches of the boys were much closer now, a constellation of floating fire stretched across the darkness. No electric torches for the Midnight Hunters—they pursued like a mob out of an old fairy tale, brandishing their flaming sticks.

"You want fire?" came Heinrich's ragged cry. "I'll give you fire!"

One of the torches arced high into the air. Still dazed, Max pushed himself to his feet and staggered onward. He was moving stiffly, and the pain in his side radiated across his back. He risked a glance over his shoulder. The thrown torch had landed squarely in one of the tomato plant shelters, and the brittle vines were crackling with flames.

He felt horribly exposed. In a moment, the rapidly spreading fire would light up the garden, and there would be no more melting into the night. There were a dozen Hitler Youth boys and one Max Hoffmann. And Heinrich had a gun.

"There he is!" Heinrich shouted. Max wasn't moving quickly enough, and his legs wouldn't obey his commands to *go faster*.

His mind grasped at absurd hopes—Albert swooping out of the shadows to scoop him up and take him to safety. Stauffenberg appearing between Max and the Hitler Youth, drawing a pistol of his own. A sudden air-raid siren splitting the night.

Of course, he was alone. Nobody was coming to help—not the resistance, not the RAF bombers. Even Gerta and Kat were too far away now.

He was going to have to save himself. Up ahead, the grass gave way to the sidewalk and street that bordered the garden's northern edge. Across the street, the ruins of bombed-out apartment blocks filtered the night sky through bare and for-lorn windows.

He hit the sidewalk at full speed, forcing his aching body into a runner's form. The safe house was southeast of here, but he didn't dare risk heading in that direction—he knew he would be dangerously exposed on the empty streets. Instead, he stayed the course, sprinting due north toward the ruins. He burst through a doorless frame and found himself in the wreckage of a small sitting room. Great chunks of fallen brick had collapsed the sofa and table. Above his head, the ceiling was pocked with massive holes. The shattered facade of the outer wall gave him a view across the street and into the garden.

He ducked down and raised his eyes to peer through a crack.

The fire had spread along the dry summer grass, turning the figures of the Hitler Youth into hazy silhouettes. He watched Heinrich leave the garden, cross the road, and draw his pistol. The boy's bright eyes scanned the ruins.

"They've got to be in there," he called to his fellow Midnight Hunters as they joined him, brandishing torches of their own.

Max's heart sank. His hiding place was obvious. He hoped Kat and Gerta were far away from here. At least then, the Midnight Hunters wouldn't get all three of them.

He had no choice but to work his way deeper into the apartment and hope the whole precarious structure didn't come tumbling down on his head. Quickly, quietly, he turned away from the cracked facade and picked his way toward the back of the sitting room.

"Come out, come out, little dragons . . ." Heinrich's voice had a singsong lilt. *He's enjoying this*, Max thought, ducking through a half-collapsed doorjamb and into a small bedroom. By now, his eyes had adjusted, and he could make out the shape of a charred and twisted crib.

"I know you're just a bunch of little kids," Heinrich called out. "You think this is playtime? This is *war*."

Amid the wreckage, it was impossible to tell how close Heinrich was getting. *Keep moving*, Max thought. One of the bedroom walls was a hollow mess of plaster and load-bearing beams. He found the widest hole and began to slip through it to the room on the other side—and knocked loose a chunk of plaster with his elbow. In the silent ruins, it might as well have been a linden tree crashing to the ground.

Max heard a muffled shout—"He's back there!"—and dove the rest of the way through the wall, nearly crying out as the corner of a beam poked his bruised rib. He had come to a dining room whose fallen chandelier had scattered bits of crystal along the floor. It was like walking on marbles. Max knew that he could find himself trapped in any of these rooms, cornered like an animal for the Midnight Hunters to toy with. But he had to keep going. His plan was to emerge from the back of the wreckage and vanish into the winding streets of Pankow. Then, when it was safe, he would double back and make his way home.

The problem was, there was no way to navigate the ruins, and he had completely lost his bearings. For all he knew, he would climb through the next broken wall and pop out into the street in front of the community garden in Prenzlauer Berg.

A loud crash came from somewhere nearby, followed by a muffled curse. He imagined those two heavyset boys trying to slip through narrow spaces. Maybe they would get stuck and seal off the route from the rest of the Hitler Youth.

That was unlikely, but he had to hope for *something*.

The dining room gave way to a corridor littered with debris, and Max scampered over piles of brick without his feet ever touching the floor. It occurred to him that he might be walking on top of buried corpses.

The corridor took him past a smashed toilet, the jagged shards of a bathtub, and a sink that was intact but lying on its side, detached from the wall. The porcelain gave off an eerie glow. Max stopped, dumbfounded. The porcelain seemed almost *alive*, as the faint glow brightened to an orange fire that swam across its smooth surface.

It was the reflection of torchlight. He crouched down next to a fallen wall. For a moment, he couldn't tell where the real light was coming from, and dizziness washed over him. It was like being in the mirrored fun house of the carnival whose tents used to sprout like brightly colored mushrooms on the banks of the Spree in summers before the war.

Then Heinrich stepped into view. Max peeked out of a tiny space between bricks. The boy was holding his pistol casually at his side, frowning intently as he moved the torch to send light into different corners of the room. Max made himself as small as he could as the light played along his hiding place. What would he do if Heinrich discovered him here? Would he try to rush the older boy, knock the pistol from his hand, at least give himself a fighting chance?

No. The risk of getting shot was too great. He knew that he wasn't brave enough to do it. He would simply give himself up.

If he had Papa's knife, things would be different.

He imagined he could feel its cool grip in his hand, metal rings shielding his knuckles.

The light seemed to creep into his hiding place, clawing at the shadows. Was Heinrich moving closer?

Max held his breath. His ribs throbbed.

And then the light receded. He waited a moment, then picked his head up and peered through the gap in the bricks.

Heinrich was gone.

Was it a trick?

He had to take the chance. He couldn't stay here all night. Being careful not to dislodge any bricks or send a shard of porcelain skittering into the wall, Max crept from the ruined bathroom. Beyond it was another collapsed hallway, open to the night sky. Max expected Heinrich's arm to dart out of the blackness at any moment. His ears were attuned to the slightest sounds. He heard the Hitler Youth boys moving about the apartment block, but their footsteps sounded muffled and distant.

Suddenly, the corridor became more rubble than hallway. There was always a between place like this, where the structure simply accepted its destruction. Max found himself looking out upon the streets of Pankow.

He crept to the very edge of the corridor and glanced from side to side. No torches in sight.

Quickly, he moved through the tall grass of what had once been neatly fenced-off yards attached to the block's ground-floor flats.

He looked behind him. There, amid the ruins, torchlight appeared through gaps in the walls, then abruptly vanished as the boys conducted their slow search of the apartment block. It looked like fireflies trapped in a sunken city.

Max crossed the road and turned a corner. The next time he glanced back, there was nothing but darkness. He ducked into a narrow alley and waited for a few minutes, keeping his eyes on the street. When he was satisfied that no one had followed him, he left the alley and headed home—dizzy, bruised, and exhausted, but alive.

SIXTEEN

JULY 15, 1944

The noonday sun did nothing to dispel the gloom of the Wolf's Lair. Seated at a table beneath an austere pine tree, Claus von Stauffenberg pushed the remnants of a late breakfast around his plate. He felt a creeping desolation in his bones. *Even the sun is repulsed by this place*, he thought, glancing around the drab, melancholy camp of concrete huts and bunkers hidden deep in Poland's Masurian woods. The atmosphere was one of eerie, tense quiet. It could be a peaceful place—it probably was, once—but the endless SS checkpoints, all those secret passwords and searching eyes, gave visitors the feeling that they were constantly being watched.

This was simply an extension of the Führer's paranoia. He had taken to wearing a bulletproof waistcoat and metal-plated cap, and Stauffenberg had heard a report that several men were garrisoned here with the sole purpose of tasting Hitler's food in case it had been poisoned.

The Valkyrie plotters believed that Hitler had gotten wind

of the conspiracy. There could be no more delays. Even without Himmler or Göring present in the briefing room, Stauffenberg had resolved to plant the bomb. Taking out the Nazi high command had proved too lofty a goal. The assassination was now solely focused on the Führer. Any other high-ranking Nazi officials would be a bonus.

Even if he weren't eating breakfast with a bomb in the briefcase at his side, Stauffenberg thought he would still be swamped by a feeling of growing dread. His stomach knotted, and he gave up on the plate of eggs and sausages.

Freedom can only be won by action, he said to himself. The simple words had become a mantra between Stauffenberg and his brother Berthold. All the poetry he had quoted to rally his aristocratic friends to his cause, the high-minded principles he had cited in defense of assassination as a necessary tactic to save millions of lives—all of it had sloughed off like dead skin as the stark reality of his role became fixed in his mind. Now he thought in the blunt phrases of his more proletarian colleagues.

There was nothing poetic about a bomb. A bomb was fire and destruction.

The poetry would come afterward, when they rebuilt a Germany free of Nazi rule. The poetry of rebirth, peace, and prosperity.

Today, he must transform himself into a blunt instrument, and it was helpful to think in equally blunt terms.

"No appetite, Colonel?"

For a brief moment, Stauffenberg feared he might lose his breakfast at the sound of Field Marshal Keitel's voice. There was a slightly mocking edge to it, as if Keitel viewed Stauffenberg's inability to finish his food as something he could use against him at a later date.

Stauffenberg forced himself to meet the man's eyes with cordial indifference. "The flight from Berlin was especially turbulent. I'm afraid my stomach isn't what it once was, ever since North Africa."

He held up his right arm, giving Keitel a good look at the empty sleeve where his hand had been.

Keitel eyed Stauffenberg's injury with poorly disguised longing, as if he wished to be the one who had heroically recovered from grievous wounds sustained in battle.

"They use too much salt here, anyway," Keitel said, with a wink. Stauffenberg had to hand it to the man—his schemes evolved so fast that he couldn't even make small talk without cycling through several different personalities at once.

The field marshal's presence was like a foul smell in a musty attic. Even outside among the pines, Stauffenberg felt stifled.

The Führer's previous base of operations, the Berghof, had at least been perched on the edge of a cliff, and the Bavarian air had been fresh and sweet—an antidote to the rot that corrupted the halls of the building itself. But here at Hitler's eastern headquarters, there was no such relief.

A harried-looking sergeant-major came rushing over to the table.

"My apologies, gentlemen—the Führer wishes to greet you outside, and then you will make your way to the briefing room together."

He gestured toward a wide pathway of packed earth. Stauffenberg's gaze swept along the attendees already gathered in front of the guest bunker—generals and admirals, mostly. Stauffenberg recognized Karl Bodenschatz from the army and Jesko von Puttkamer from the navy. High-ranking military members whose deaths would have little impact on the Valkyrie coup one way or another. Still, they were all Nazi supporters who loved their Führer. Stauffenberg put their deaths out of his mind. Anyone here at the Wolf's Lair was an acceptable casualty, as long as the Führer was killed. Including Stauffenberg himself, if it came to that.

Stauffenberg and Keitel followed the sergeant-major along the pathway. Mentally, he rehearsed the plan. The day's agenda called for a presentation on the Allied progress in France, followed by a second presentation on the Russian advance along the Eastern Front. There would be a short break between the sessions, which gave Stauffenberg the perfect opportunity to arm the bomb in his briefcase without arousing suspicion. He would set the case down as close to Hitler as possible, then excuse himself to make an urgent phone call to Berlin.

He would then leave the visitors' bunker and hurry across

the grounds of the Wolf's Lair to the signal shelter. There, he would wait for the explosion alongside General Erich Fellgiebel, a coconspirator. After the bomb exploded, Fellgiebel would give the orders to activate Valkyrie and then cut off the Wolf's Lair from any further outside communications.

Finally, Stauffenberg's aide-de-camp, Werner von Haeften, would drive Stauffenberg through the checkpoints and out of the Wolf's Lair as quickly as possible. Then it was back to the airfield and off to Berlin, where the difficult work of coordinating Operation Valkyrie would begin.

"I said, he is looking well today," Keitel said, apparently for the second time. Stauffenberg had been too distracted by his plan to notice that the field marshal was speaking to him.

"Who?" Stauffenberg said.

Keitel paused and gave Stauffenberg a curious sidelong glance. "The Führer, of course. Did that turbulent plane ride knock something loose in your brain, Claus?"

Keitel's false camaraderie raised a faint alarm in Stauffenberg's mind. And was it just Stauffenberg's imagination, or was Keitel giving his briefcase a long appraisal?

They took their places among the guests while Hitler worked his way down the row, clasping hands. Stauffenberg noted the way Hitler's leg still dragged. Contrary to Keitel's opinion, he was not looking well at all. His face was puffy and his posture hunched. To stop himself from staring, Stauffenberg shifted his gaze to the visitors' bunker. It was an ugly concrete block of a building with vegetation planted on its roof as camouflage against bombers. It brought to mind some impossibly huge mushroom that had sprouted from the forest floor, topped with flak guns instead of a squishy cap.

Stauffenberg stood at attention, then offered the three remaining fingers on his left hand for the Führer to shake. He met Hitler's watery eyes for a moment, and something passed between the two men—an odd sensation that reminded Stauffenberg of the way his wife, Nina, described her migraine headaches beginning with a sort of aura, a vague sense that the atmosphere had shifted slightly.

How strange, Stauffenberg thought, *that Hitler is an arm's length away from the instrument of his destruction.* If he were to demand to see the contents of the briefcase right now, Stauffenberg would be tortured and shot before the afternoon was out.

While the Führer's fingers still gripped his own, all that could go wrong with the plan nearly brought Stauffenberg to his knees. What were the chances that Haeften could get them safely through the SS checkpoints after the bomb went off?

Everything depended on swiftness of action.

With the same willpower he had called upon to recover from his injuries, Stauffenberg blanked his mind. He gave Hitler a short respectful bow, and the Führer dropped his hand and moved on to Keitel.

Stauffenberg maintained his focus for the next hour, taking in relevant information and ignoring everything else. The briefing room was in the basement of the visitors' bunker—a hollow cube with concrete walls and a single long table cluttered with maps. With no windows for the shock wave to escape, the blast would be contained, its explosive power magnified. The briefing room was the perfect death trap. Stauffenberg couldn't have designed it any better.

Finally, after so many false starts, things were beginning to fall into place.

When the first session ended and refreshments were being served, Stauffenberg excused himself and walked calmly down the hall to the washroom. Inside, he set the briefcase down on a small table and retrieved his special pliers from their pocket, using the stump at the end of his right arm for leverage as he undid the buckles. Then he opened the case and removed a small parcel wrapped in white cloth. Inside the parcel, explosives the size of two large chocolate bars awaited the fuse that would ignite them.

Stauffenberg picked up the fuse—a metal rod encasing a vial of sulfuric acid—and willed his hand to stop trembling. If he mishandled the fuse, the bomb would be useless. Slowly, he slid the fuse into a slot at the top of the bomb's thin casing. Then he took his special pliers and paused with their teeth gripping the fuse. Once he squeezed the pliers and clipped the vial inside the rod, there would be no going back. The bomb would be armed and the countdown would begin.

For Germany, he thought. *For the world.*

He squeezed the pliers, putting a deep crimp in the fuse and breaking the vial inside. He wrapped up the bomb and placed it back in his briefcase. He couldn't help but wonder about the supposed ten-minute fuse. Would the summer heat affect the timing? What if he only had seven minutes? Or five?

He used a hand towel to dab sweat from his face, smoothed the front of his uniform, and exited the washroom. The corridor was empty. That was good. That meant that the second briefing session was just beginning.

He nodded to the SS guard beside the door, tucked the briefcase under his arm, and reached for the handle. With a start, the guard moved quickly to pull open the door for Stauffenberg.

He stepped into the briefing room and scanned the fifteen or twenty men gathered around the table, chatting among themselves. Hitler had not yet returned. That gave Stauffenberg a moment to situate himself and find the ideal place to set the briefcase down.

"Better than the breakfast, eh?" Keitel said, stuffing a big piece of apple strudel into his mouth as Stauffenberg passed by.

He returned the greetings of the military men of his acquaintance and walked to the center of the table, slightly to the left of where Hitler had stood to preside over the earlier briefing. He set the case down and gave it a slight nudge with the toe of his boot. He wanted it out of sight, but he didn't want its explosive charge dampened by the table—although it probably wouldn't matter. The windowless room would amplify the bomb's power. Everyone in here would be killed instantly.

By that time, God willing, Stauffenberg would be in Haeften's car, making for the airfield.

Suddenly, the door swung open and the chatter ceased. Hitler's personal secretary, Martin Bormann, filled the door frame with his bulk.

"Gentlemen," he said. "With regret, I must inform you that the Führer has been called away on a most urgent matter. He has requested that the briefing session continue in his absence. Good day to you."

Bormann backed out into the hallway, pulling the door shut.

Stauffenberg stared after Bormann in disbelief. While his mind reeled, his body felt impossibly heavy, his feet rooted to the floor. The words of his mantra came and went.

Freedom

Action

He had to make a decision. Leave the bomb where it was and let it explode, killing a few Nazis, yes—but not Himmler, Göring, or Hitler himself—or take the bomb back to the washroom and attempt to disarm it himself.

Keitel turned to him. "Well, then, Colonel, why don't we bump your update to the top of the agenda."

He felt twenty pairs of eyes settle on his face.

Say something, Claus!

He opened his mouth. He was so thirsty, his words were going to crumble in his throat and come out as dust. How long had it been since he'd armed the bomb? Three minutes? Four?

He had no idea.

"My apologies," he said, trying to keep his voice strong and clear, his tone casual and light. "But I need a moment to prepare my notes." He bent to pick up his briefcase. This would strike some of the men in the room as unprofessional and out of character for Stauffenberg, but he had to make the bluff work.

Keitel frowned. "Your reports are always exemplary, Colonel. I'm sure we won't mind a more cursory update, in the interest of keeping the briefing moving."

Stauffenberg couldn't wait for Keitel's permission. He strode toward the door. "Excuse me," he said, sounding every inch the aristocrat, "I'll just be a moment."

He felt Keitel's eyes boring into him. The man seemed about to say something else, and Stauffenberg knew he was weighing the prospect of giving Stauffenberg a command to save face.

"We'll begin with the Eastern Front, then," he said, turning back to the men at the table.

Stauffenberg opened the door, stepped out into the hall, and let the SS guard shut the door behind him. His heart was fluttering and he felt his pulse in his throat. Briefly, the absurd thought entered his mind that the briefcase had suddenly become transparent, and the SS man could see the bomb.

Inside the washroom he locked the door, placed the briefcase on the table, and removed the wrapped parcel. The stale air seemed to lack oxygen. He held the bomb steady against the table with his stump, clamped the fuse between the knuckles of his first and second fingers—and pulled. The fuse did not budge. With a second hand, it would be no trouble to pry the metal rod loose, but his stump did not provide enough leverage.

Stauffenberg removed the pliers from the briefcase and affixed them to his fingers. Holding his breath, he clamped the teeth of the pliers down on the fuse, careful not to put another crimp in the metal. He didn't want to accelerate the work of the acid. Slowly, he slid the fuse out of its slot in the bomb's casing. At the last second, he paused. Would manually separating the fuse from the explosives trigger the bomb? He had no idea if he was doing this properly. He had not planned on ever having to disarm it.

He closed his eyes and thought of Nina and the children, fixing their faces in his mind. Then he tore the fuse away from the casing.

For a moment, he stood perfectly still. Then he opened his eyes.

The explosives lay on the table. The fuse was wedged between the pliers' teeth.

Relief surged through him. He let out a long breath and stared at his trembling hand as if it were an alien appendage.

Hitler and I and our shaky hands! he thought wildly. Water. He needed a drink of water. He had never been so thirsty.

There was water in the briefing room, sweating metal pitchers of ice-cold water.

Still trembling, he shoved the bomb and the pliers into his briefcase. He placed the dead fuse in the side pocket, counted backward from ten, and left the washroom, mentally rehearsing his presentation on the state of the Reserve Army.

SEVENTEEN

The moonlight tastes like salt.

Kat Vogel remembered the night her mother told her that she could taste the moonlight as a little girl, but as she got older and became a grown woman, she lost the ability.

It's because the moonlight controls the tides, and the ocean is very salty.

Kat crossed the street, moving in and out of the camouflage netting strung from sidewalk to sidewalk. Tonight, the skies were clear and moonlight bathed Prenzlauer Berg in a pale glow. She thought of the dreamy look in her mother's eyes when she recalled her own childhood in the Bavarian countryside. Kat used to think of her mother as a wood sprite, a free spirit connected to the natural world in ways that Kat, as a child of the city, would never understand.

Everyone thought of her parents as an odd couple: the ethereal woman who could calm a frightened horse with a whispered word, and the blustery Wehrmacht general who spent his days playing politics in smoky government briefing rooms.

But Kat saw what the others didn't see. At home in their spacious flat, her parents' personalities fit together like puzzle pieces, forming an unlikely whole that made perfect sense in the end.

And now that puzzle was forever undone.

She moved swiftly, averting her eyes as she passed a drunken couple swaying and giggling as they walked. It was very late, but the full moon and the mild weather had brought a few sleepless citizens out into the streets.

It was too painful to think of her father's half of the puzzle. Words like *torture* and *execution*—words Karl and Ingrid Hoffmann whispered when they thought she couldn't hear— were almost beyond what she was able to imagine. When she lay awake in her bed at night ambushed by thoughts of her father's fate, she tapped out a two-fingered rhythm on her palm. Eventually, the swells and crests of some imaginary jazz band— American jazz, not the watered-down, Nazi-approved German jazz they played on the radio now—chased the dark thoughts away.

Her mother was another matter entirely. She was alive, and her spirit, which had never seemed tethered to her body any- way, was present in everything Kat saw, heard, and touched. She hoped that wherever her mother was, there were trees.

As she took a sharp right at the end of the street, she felt her pulse begin to pound with the most familiar rhythm of all.

Rage.

The pure, undistilled anger that had driven her to throw rocks at the Hitler Youth and a brick through the window of their headquarters.

Max thought she was too reckless. Gerta did, too, although she hid her feelings better than her brother. But the Becker Circle had been careful, hadn't they? And in the end, despite their caution, they had been taken down—captured, killed, or forced into hiding.

Her father dead. Her mother a captive.

Kat accepted that it wasn't fair to put the Hoffmanns in danger with her actions. That's why tonight's mission was for Kat alone. She would tell Max and Gerta about it in the morning, after the item had been secured. Then they could decide if they were in or out for the next phase of attack against the Hitler Youth.

Now, where was the house? She paused beneath the awning of a boarded-up hat shop. It should be just up ahead, at the bend in the road. Yes! There it was. The building with the most ornate facade on the street gave way to the wealthiest section of the whole district—carriage houses set comfortably back from the traffic, complete with their own garages. There was a house at the very end of the block with a gabled roof and well-kept shrubbery. On one of the Red Dragons' trips to the community garden she had seen an automobile pull out of its garage. It was a Mercedes-Benz, the car of a wealthy citizen, like a Nazi functionary or an industrialist.

The Red Dragons needed something better than absinthe to burn.

Cars needed fuel to run.

The math was simple.

Kat waited beneath the awning, flattening herself against the boarded-up window as a pair of older gentlemen passed by, whispering intently about the fighting in France. When they were out of sight, she stepped out into the moonlight, dashed across the street and down the block.

She slowed as she reached the house. Attached to one side was the low-slung brick hut of the garage. She ducked behind a hedgerow and moved around the side of the house until she found what she was looking for: a single square window in the garage.

She kept going until she found a gap in the hedgerow she could slip through, then doubled back to the window. She had a small electric torch in her pocket, but didn't dare use it until she was inside the garage. She felt along the windowsill, pressed her hands against the base of the window, and pushed upward. To her great relief, it wasn't locked. It was a small window, too small for an adult burglar to slip through.

They hadn't counted on someone as slight as Kat Vogel.

When she had raised it as high as it would go, stretching her arms up above her head, she pulled her hands away from the window.

It slammed shut with a loud *BANG*.

Kat scrambled down into the dirt beneath the hedgerow, cursing herself. She watched the house, waiting for narrow bands of light to appear behind the blacked-out windows.

Several minutes passed. Just as she was about to creep from the shelter of the hedgerow, the sound of a door opening made her freeze. Footsteps came across the cobblestones of the front walk, and then stopped. She could just barely make out a solitary figure in the darkness, clothed in a dressing gown. For all Kat knew, he was staring right at her hiding place.

The man stayed like this, motionless, and Kat imagined he was listening intently to the sounds of the city, trying to identify what had torn him from sleep. She kept very still, taking slow, silent breaths. After a while, the man went back into the house. Kat waited another few minutes, then began searching the dirt beneath the hedgerow until she found what she was looking for: a long stick.

With the stick in hand, she went to the window, slid it open, and wedged the stick between the sill and the bottom of the raised window. It didn't feel very secure, but it would have to do. Careful not to disturb the stick, she hoisted herself up and over the windowsill and into the garage, landing on a cement floor.

The garage was pitch-black and smelled of oil. She had to risk using her torch. When she clicked it on, the beam illuminated the shiny passenger door of the wine-colored Mercedes. The owner of the car clearly took very good care of it. The vehicle was buffed to a high sheen.

Rage tapped out its skittering rhythm in her mind.

The urge to find something sharp to scratch the car with was nearly unbearable. She imagined how satisfying it would feel to flake off the paint with a nail, etching a red dragon into the door.

Kat banished the thought to focus on the mission at hand. The beam of her torch played along shelves holding all manner of odds and ends—wrenches, gardening tools, a bicycle seat. Next to the shelves were buckets of paint, neatly stacked, along with a few silver canisters the size of soup cans.

She knelt down and examined them. Each canister was labeled *Benzin*—gasoline. With Germany's wartime oil shortage, scientists had rushed to create alternative sources of fuel to power the Wehrmacht's tanks and the Luftwaffe's planes. Like ersatz bread and coffee, it worked well enough but was no substitute for the real thing. That was okay. Kat didn't need to start the engine of a Panzer tank. She just needed something that burned bright and hot.

She picked up one of the canisters. It was heavier than it looked. Liquid sloshed around inside.

There were seven canisters of ersatz fuel. Would the owner notice if some of them were missing? Her gut told her that three was too many to steal. She would settle for two. Even a small amount of fuel was a million times better than a dusty bottle of absinthe.

She unfolded a small cloth bag she'd jammed into her pocket. She set two canisters into the bag and bundled it tight to keep them from knocking together. Then she went to the window, leaned out, and dropped the bag softly into the grass. Careful not to disturb the stick, she climbed through the propped-open window and landed outside next to her bag. She paused for a moment, pressed against the outside wall of the garage, listening. Nothing seemed out of the ordinary. With one hand supporting the underside of the window, she pulled the stick away and quickly tossed it aside so that she could support the window with two hands. Then she lowered it down softly.

Bag in hand, she slipped through the gap in the hedgerow and headed for home.

EIGHTEEN

The Americans have taken the town of Saint-Lô," Mutti said. She slid a map of France across the table, full of squiggly lines and tiny print, which Max had to squint to read.

"Mutti," Gerta said, "did you *make* this?"

"Ingrid has become quite the cartographer," Papa said, munching on a crumbly biscuit.

"It passes the time," Mutti said. "But look!" She passed the map pointedly to Kat. "They're making progress."

It was the evening of July 19. Six weeks had passed since the Allied landings on the beaches of Normandy. If the map of France was the size of a hand, it looked like the Allies had advanced the length of a thumbnail. The town of Saint-Lô was on the little spit of land that jutted out into the English Channel. The Allies were still hundreds of kilometers from Paris, thousands of kilometers from Berlin.

To Max's surprise, Kat actually studied the map with interest and agreed with Mutti—or at least pretended to. "I'm sure they're going as fast as they can," she said, passing the paper back across the table.

For the last few days, Kat had been in suspiciously high spirits, flitting in and out of Max's room, tapping out a quick rhythm on his shoulders, humming to herself. Something was going on, but whatever it was, she hadn't shared it with him.

He lifted his spoon from his watery stew and bit into a parsnip. Oh, how he missed the kitchen garden at the villa in Dahlem! These vegetables the communist underground delivered were always the runts of the litter, shriveled and tasteless.

He forced himself to chew, swallow, and take another bite without making a face. He knew what Mutti would say: *We are lucky to have anything at all.*

Except these days, he thought, she probably wouldn't notice if he dumped the bowl of stew over his sister's head. He watched his mother as she ignored her own food, bent to her map, and shaded in a little piece of French territory with the stub of a pencil.

"Ingrid," Papa said.

"Karl," she muttered, blackening the line.

Papa's hand settled gently over Mutti's. Only then did she stop working on the map and look up. She blinked as if seeing her husband for the first time. Then she glanced around the table.

"Sorry," she said with a weak smile. "I've been getting a little carried away."

"Maybe we need a night away from the radio," Papa suggested.

"Maybe you could use a little fresh air," Gerta said cautiously.

Mutti put down her pencil and straightened her posture. "We are to *stay inside*. I don't know what's so difficult to understand about that."

Max was relieved to see his mother's old spark return, even for a moment. Lately she had been little more than a ghost, haunting the radio dials and working on her maps.

"Brave people have *sacrificed* to keep us alive and out of the camps," she continued. "It's our responsibility to respect the danger that we're in, not to increase it by being reckless." She peered intently at Gerta, then at Kat. "Where do you go, when you sneak out at night?"

Max froze with his spoon halfway to his mouth.

Mutti laughed. "Did you think I didn't know?"

"Ingrid," Papa said softly.

"*Karl.*" She looked at Max. "Your father thinks you are little adults. He's forgotten that you are the children and we are the parents."

"You're not my parents," Kat said. There was no malice in her voice; she was simply stating a fact.

"Be that as it may, we are responsible for your safety," Mutti said. "I have let this go on for far too long. From now on, you are to stay inside at night, in your beds, sleeping."

"We just went out a few times to get some air," Kat said. "That's all."

Mutti laughed again, though Max didn't think she found this very funny. "I was your age once, too, Kat." She sighed. "I know this is hard. Every night before I fall asleep I lie there thinking that it's monstrously unfair that you have to spend your childhood dodging bombs and hiding indoors. But—"

"So many people have it so much worse," Gerta finished the thought.

"Yes," Mutti said. She smiled sadly. "You see how repetitive I am these days. How boring. Just like our mornings and our afternoons. But all I want is for us to hold on to what we have."

Papa kissed her on the cheek. After they had finished eating, Max, Gerta, and Kat cleared the table and washed the dishes while Papa and Mutti settled in beside the radio. Evidently, Papa's suggestion of a night off from the broadcasts had been forgotten.

Upstairs, Max retreated into his room for the night. He was suddenly very tired. The safe house could simmer for days without his parents saying much of anything. When Mutti suddenly laid her feelings bare, there was a special rawness to it that made him vaguely ashamed.

Kat and Gerta followed him into his room.

"I don't want to hear it," he said. "I just want to go to bed."

"Listen to me," Kat said quietly, curling her fingers around his arm. "I got us some fuel."

"What? How did you do that?"

The absurd notion of Kat walking into a store and plunking down a pile of Reichsmarks came and went.

"It doesn't matter," she said. "The point is, now we can really burn the Midnight Hunters!"

"I'm not burning anybody!" Max said.

"She means burn down their stupid headquarters," Gerta said. "The hunting lodge. Right?"

"Oh," Kat said, letting Max's arm go. "Right. I mean we can burn down the hunting lodge."

Max turned to his sister. "Did you not hear what Mutti just said?"

"This will be the last time," Gerta said. "Promise."

He looked from Gerta to Kat. Both of the girls' eyes shone with the same kind of inner fire. Mutti's words hadn't meant a thing to them. They were swept up in the Red Dragons, in the excitement of their missions, in the promise of fire and blood.

Max opened his mouth to remind them that last time he'd almost been caught by the Midnight Hunters, and it was only through sheer luck that he'd been able to slip away into the night.

"If we don't do this," Gerta said quickly, "if we let the Red Dragons just disappear, then Heinrich wins. The Hitler Youth win. They'll think they scared us off for good."

"We came this far," Kat said. "Now we just have to finish it."

Max thought of Mutti downstairs, bent over her map,

charting Allied troop movements. Was it his imagination, or was she turning even paler than usual? Her skin had a sickly pallor.

Maybe they were all going crazy in their own ways.

He took a deep breath. "Okay, but after tonight, I'm done."

Kat clapped him on the shoulder. "Last ride of the Red Dragons."

NINETEEN

The knife in Max's pocket weighed as much as an elephant, a Panzer tank, a Lancaster bomber. He felt it with every step. Its hilt stuck out so far that he untucked his shirt to hide it. He thought it would be obvious to anyone if it wasn't pitch-black on the streets of Berlin.

It had been a simple matter to slip into Mutti and Papa's room while they were downstairs listening to the radio. As before, the knife was in the drawer in the nightstand. This time, Max took it back to his own room, where he slid the blade all the way out of the scabbard and carefully tested the edge.

It was very sharp.

Now, as they turned onto Stargader Strasse—Kat in the lead, Gerta following, Max bringing up the rear—he wished he had put the knife back in Papa's nightstand. He didn't want to stab anybody. He didn't think he *could* stab anybody, not even Heinrich, not even in self-defense. And besides, a street fight would bring the Gestapo running . . .

Then again, so would bombs.

Kat had made them in the back hallway of the safe house, working by the light of Gerta's small torch. She had scavenged three small glass bottles of unknown liquid from a dusty cabinet, dumped the liquid in the sink, and filled the bottles with foul-smelling ersatz fuel from two silver canisters. Then she had stuffed strips of torn bed linen into the top of each bottle and stoppered them so that the linen stuck out like a kite tail.

This was the wick. All they had to do, Kat said, was put a match to the wick, set the linen on fire, and hurl the bottles into the hunting lodge. As soon as the glass shattered, the fuel would spray everywhere, igniting and spreading the flames.

Kat was carrying the bombs in a small bag stuffed with a towel so the bottles wouldn't knock together. Gerta was carrying the matches.

And I have the knife, he thought, following the girls down the empty street. Dense clouds hid the moon, and he could just barely make out the spire of the Gethsemane Church. The saint was shrouded in darkness.

Kat came to a sudden halt. Across the street, where the low-slung buildings flanked the hunting lodge, a tiny orange dot floated in the air. It glowed brighter for a moment, then plummeted to the ground and winked out.

"A match," Kat whispered. That was all she needed to say. Max knew what it meant: One of the Midnight Hunters was outside guarding the group's headquarters.

"We need to distract him," Gerta said.

Even in the dark, Max could feel the eyes of both girls on him. He sighed. "Fine. I'll go to the end of the block and do . . . something."

"What?" Gerta said.

Max had no idea. "You'll know when it happens. As soon as he comes over to see what's going on, throw the bombs and run back the way we came. I'll circle around and meet you at home."

"Okay," Kat said. "Gerta, the second the guard moves, light the wicks."

Gerta touched his arm. "Luck be with you, Hornet."

"I don't need luck, Wasp." And with that, Max was off, hurrying to the end of the block.

The best distraction would be to shout wildly for help. That would probably bring the boy running, along with every policeman in Prenzlauer Berg. He had to make just enough noise to draw the guard away from his post, but not enough to wake up the neighborhood.

When he judged that he was about twenty or thirty paces away from the boy, he stopped. Kat and Gerta were nowhere to be seen, concealed by the moonless night. But the boy lit another match, and Max watched the orange dot hover in the darkness.

Gerta's parting words had given him an idea. He knew the triumphant *Hornet and Wasp* theme song by heart—a galloping tune sung by a choir of men with deep, powerful voices. He cleared his throat and began to sing.

"When . . . there's . . . trouble afoot down in old London town—"

The orange dot spiraled to the ground. "Who's there?" the guard hissed.

"And the crim-in-al element's taunting the crown—"

"Reinhardt, is that you?" the guard's voice drew closer. Max took a few steps back, leading the boy as far as he could from his post before it was time to take off running.

"Two heroes stand tall—"

The boy was close enough for Max to see a vague shape in the night coming toward him. Max kept backpedaling.

"Where others may fall—"

"Show yourself!" the boy said.

"It's Hornet! Hornet! Hornet and Wasp!"

"Heinrich!" the boy called out. "They're here!"

Max nearly froze in his tracks. Had the Red Dragons just walked into a trap? He opened his mouth to scream at Gerta and Kat to *run—*

Torches blinked on up and down the street.

At the same time, a ball of flame soared through the air, searing a bright arc into the darkness. The bottle-bomb crashed through the window. A radiant flash lit up the street, and in that instant Max glimpsed a dozen Hitler Youth boys swarming their headquarters.

Kat and Gerta were surrounded.

Flames shot out of the broken window and began to lap at the awning of the bakery next door.

The boy who yelled for Heinrich abandoned his hunt for Max and turned back toward his burning headquarters.

The whole street erupted in shouting. Torchlights waved in wild patterns as the boys ran to save their hunting lodge. Above the din, Heinrich's voice rang out loud and clear.

"Don't let them get away!"

Max hoped that Gerta and Kat had the sense to drop the two unexploded bombs and run for their lives. He turned his back on the chaotic scene, sprinted toward a bend in Stargader Strasse, and slammed into something that knocked him off his feet.

Dazed, he went to his knees and started to push himself up, when a meaty hand grabbed his arm. He was hit by the smell of onions and mustard. A face loomed in the darkness. Firelight flashed across a pair of spectacles.

"Gerhard!" Max said, flooded with relief. "It's me, remember? I helped you after those boys beat you up in the garden."

"I remember," Gerhard said. He tightened his grip on Max's arm.

"Listen, I really need to get going," Max said. He tried to stand up, but Gerhard shoved him back down.

"Gerhard," Max said, "I'm your friend."

"You're a Red Dragon," Gerhard said. Max's eyes swept across the boy's crisp brown uniform. He moved his shirttail aside and clasped the hilt of the knife.

"Heinrich!" Gerhard's cry was piercing and shrill.

"Shhh!" Max said. "You don't have to do this!"

Gerhard hesitated. Then he yelled even louder. "Heinrich, I caught one of them! Over here!"

Max pulled the knife out of his pocket, unsheathed the blade, and held it up to Gerhard's belly. Gerhard yelped in surprise, released Max's arm, and raised both hands above his head. Max got to his feet.

"I felt sorry for you," Max said. "But you're nothing but a Nazi."

Suddenly, something cold and metallic pressed into the back of Max's head. Heinrich's voice in his ear sent a chill down his spine: "And you're a traitor to your race."

"Heinrich!" Gerhard cried happily. "I found him!"

"Very good work, Gerhard. You can put your hands down now. I'll take it from here."

Gerhard eyed the knife and hesitated.

"I'll cut him up," Max warned. It didn't sound very convincing.

Heinrich laughed. "With such a shaky hand?"

Max winced as Heinrich pressed the barrel of his pistol hard into the back of his head. "Drop the knife, *now.*"

Max's thoughts raced, but there was nothing he could do.

He couldn't outrun a bullet. Heinrich would shoot him before he moved a muscle.

The siren of a Berlin fire brigade truck began to wail.

Max lowered his arm and let his father's knife clatter to the ground. His only hope was that Gerta and Kat had managed to slip away. He felt strangely unafraid—almost reckless—as he turned to face the leader of the Midnight Hunters. It was as if he was watching himself from a short distance away.

Heinrich lowered his own weapon, just a little, so that the gun was pointed at Max's chest rather than his head. "So sad to see one so young brainwashed by the enemies of the Fatherland."

Over Heinrich's shoulder, Max could see flames erupting from the broken windows of the hunting lodge. One of the Hitler Youth boys ran up to the building with a bucket and tossed water on the blaze. It did nothing to douse the fire. Gerta and Kat were nowhere to be seen.

"Hey," Max said, "your clubhouse is on fire."

Heinrich shrugged. "It's just a building. The Hitler Youth is a movement that transcends—"

"Oh, shut up," Max said.

Heinrich smiled. Then he smashed his pistol into the side of Max's head, catching him squarely on the temple.

Heinrich's face receded to a distant point of light. Then the world went dark.

TWENTY

JULY 20, 1944

Claus von Stauffenberg was soaked in sweat. His uniform shirt clung to his body. Wet strands of hair were plastered to his forehead. He was suffering through an interminable morning meeting with Field Marshal Keitel and two officers of the general staff.

Keitel had insisted on holding the meeting outside, under the same tall and vaguely hostile tree that Stauffenberg ate breakfast beneath on his last visit to the Wolf's Lair. Keitel obviously enjoyed Stauffenberg's discomfort. Not that it would be much cooler inside the visitors' bunker. His conference with the Führer, immediately after this meeting, was going to be stifling.

Of course, if all went according to plan, Stauffenberg would be in the room for only a minute or two. But when had anything gone according to plan for the Valkyrie plotters? He prayed that someday they would look back on all their false starts and failures from a place of peace and prosperity. Then he would be able to raise a glass to their cursed luck, safe in the knowledge that it had all worked out fine in the end.

Stauffenberg admonished himself for indulging in this pleasant fantasy. He had to stay alert and focus on his task, despite the heat and the presence of the odious Keitel.

Since his last visit to the Wolf's Lair, a friend at the Abwehr— the Wehrmacht's military intelligence service—had informed him that rumors were swirling about a plot to blow up the Führer's headquarters. To the SS, rumors were as good as fact. People had been executed based on flimsier evidence.

If the SS started rounding up the conspirators, it would be too late for any of them. All their hard work—along with the sacrifices of so many resistance fighters—would be in vain.

Today had to be the day.

". . . and the butcher said, 'But my dear *fräulein*, the eyes are for the stew!'" Keitel looked around the table. Stauffenberg blinked. Apparently, the man had just finished telling a joke. The officers of the general staff laughed politely. Stauffenberg managed a smile.

"Well," Keitel said, standing up and placing his palms on the table, "I suppose I'll see you gentlemen shortly." He lowered his voice. "The Führer is in a bad mood today. Don't say I didn't warn you."

Stauffenberg headed for the visitors' bunker. It had only been five days since his last visit, but he could swear that the foliage camouflaging the concrete building had thickened considerably. It looked as if the forest were reclaiming the Wolf's Lair for itself. On the way, he passed his aide-de-camp, Werner von Haeften, leaning against his staff car. He gave his friend a nod. Haeften picked up a briefcase from the back seat and fell in beside him.

At the entrance to the bunker, Stauffenberg spoke to the sergeant-major. "I'll need a place to wash up and change my shirt before meeting with the Führer. I look like I've fallen into the Spree."

Silently, he thanked Keitel for his pettiness. By taking such pleasure in seeing Stauffenberg sweat, he had given him the perfect excuse.

"Yes, Colonel," the sergeant-major said. He hesitated, giving Haeften a quick appraisal.

Stauffenberg held up his empty sleeve. "The lieutenant will assist me. I don't want my personal ministrations to make me late for the meeting."

The sergeant-major averted his eyes. "Of course, sir. This way."

Stauffenberg expected the man to lead them downstairs, into the cellar of the visitors' bunker, to the small washroom that he used on his last visit. Instead, the sergeant-major stopped at a wooden door just down the hall from the entrance.

"Thank you," Stauffenberg said. "I'll meet the others downstairs when I've made myself presentable."

"Oh," the sergeant-major said, "I'm sorry—weren't you

informed? The Führer has moved the meeting to the map room next door."

Stauffenberg cursed silently, struggling to keep his face composed. Why even bother to make plans, when God seemed so intent on thwarting them? Unlike the concrete briefing room in the basement of the visitors' bunker—the perfect place to plant the bomb—the map room was airy and spacious. Worse, there were several windows.

"No one told me," Stauffenberg said.

"The Führer insists that the windows help make the heat more bearable," the sergeant-major said.

"I'm sure the Führer is correct," Stauffenberg said. Haeften opened the door to the washroom and the two men stepped inside. Stauffenberg noticed that the sergeant-major was still standing just outside the door as Haeften closed it. He waited until he heard the man's footsteps fade down the hall, then set his briefcase down on a bare wooden table. Haeften did the same with the briefcase he carried and began removing two linen-wrapped parcels.

Quickly and deftly, Stauffenberg used his three working fingers to take off his uniform jacket, unbutton the sodden dress shirt underneath, and peel it away from his body. He pulled a dry, neatly folded shirt from his briefcase and put it on while Haeften unwrapped the two bombs.

Over the past few days, Stauffenberg had refined the assassination plan. This afternoon he would plant two bombs instead of one, to multiply the power of the blast. It had proved to be a wise choice—perhaps the second bomb would make up for the map room's less-than-ideal design.

Haeften was fishing for the fuses in the side pocket of his briefcase when the washroom door began to open and the sergeant-major's voice interrupted their work.

"Excuse me, gentlemen, but—"

Haeften lunged for the door, slamming it shut in the sergeant-major's face. "The colonel isn't dressed!"

"I'm sorry," the sergeant-major said through the door, "but the Führer has insisted that we begin the briefing."

Stauffenberg put on his jacket. It would not do to leave Hitler waiting. The Führer, in his short-tempered wrath, could easily have Stauffenberg barred from attending, leaving him holding an armed bomb on the wrong side of a locked door.

"We're coming!" Stauffenberg called. Haeften looked at him helplessly. Stauffenberg held up one finger.

Haeften went back to his briefcase, retrieved the fuse, and then promptly dropped the pair of pliers on the floor.

"Gentlemen, I must insist!" the sergeant-major said, pounding on the door. "The Führer has personally instructed me to—"

"One. Moment. Sergeant-Major," Stauffenberg said firmly. Haeften recovered the pliers, crimped the fuse to break the vial of acid, and carefully inserted the fuse into the slot in the bomb's casing. He handed the armed bomb to Stauffenberg, who slid it into his own briefcase and buckled it shut. Haeften packed the unarmed bomb, then turned down the collar of Stauffenberg's jacket and quickly smoothed the front of his shirt.

The two men shook hands. Stauffenberg opened the washroom door. The sergeant-major looked very nervous.

Stauffenberg remembered Keitel's words: *The Führer is in a bad mood today.* The sergeant-major probably feared for his life.

Outside the visitors' bunker, Haeften made his way to the staff car while Stauffenberg and the sergeant-major walked briskly to the map room. It was a wooden hut, much more inviting than the visitors' bunker, with three large windows in the north wall.

At the door, the SS guard stepped aside and the sergeant-major accompanied Stauffenberg inside the room, no doubt to show the Führer that he had personally retrieved the colonel, as ordered. But the briefing had already begun and none of the two dozen officers and Nazi functionaries present paid the new arrivals any mind.

General Heusinger, Hitler's assistant chief of staff, was speaking. The Führer and most of the men were leaning over the table to get a better look at an enormous map of the Eastern Front, upon which Heusinger was tapping a long wooden pointer.

"Third Panzer Army is engaged in a strategic retreat along the Lithuanian front," he said, and then paused to let everyone consider the map.

As Stauffenberg made his way past Keitel, the field marshal

broke the silence. "Perhaps when General Heusinger has finished, Colonel Stauffenberg might grace us with his report on the status of the Reserve Army. I don't believe you've had a chance to hear that yet, my Führer."

Hitler glanced up from the map. He looked as if he hadn't slept in several days. His eyes wandered to Stauffenberg, then back to Keitel. He nodded and turned his attention back to the Eastern Front.

Stauffenberg found an empty space off to the Führer's right. He set his briefcase on the floor and used the toe of his boot to slide it partially under the table.

How long did he have? Six minutes? Five?

General Heusinger cleared his throat and began to describe Third Panzer Army's situation in more detail.

Stauffenberg turned to the Wehrmacht officer to his right, a man he had never met in his life. He spoke just loud enough for a few others to hear, but not loud enough to disrupt Heusinger's briefing.

"If you'll excuse me," Stauffenberg said, "I have to make an urgent telephone call to Berlin."

The officer nodded, his attention never wavering from the map of the Eastern Front.

Stauffenberg headed quickly for the door. When he moved past Keitel, the field marshal's hand reached out to clutch his elbow.

Keitel didn't speak—he simply frowned and looked

Stauffenberg up and down. Stauffenberg felt connected by some unbreakable, invisible thread to the briefcase he'd left under the table. Keitel's eyes bored into him.

"I'll return at once," Stauffenberg said, firmly breaking Keitel's grip. Keitel opened his mouth to say something, then glanced over at Hitler, who was watching the exchange.

Stauffenberg walked to the door under Hitler's dead-eyed, inscrutable gaze. Expecting to hear the Führer bark an order to remain at the table, Stauffenberg prepared himself to stand next to a live bomb ticking down the final minutes, and then the final seconds, of his life.

He vowed to look out the window and think of Nina and the children. He didn't want the faces of these men to be the last he'd ever see.

At the door, he almost paused and glanced back over his shoulder, but he forced himself to push it open.

No one ordered him back inside. He shut the door behind him and tried to look vaguely irritated, like a man bustling about on some irksome errand. The SS guard made no move to stop him.

He felt the weight of the briefcase at his side like the phantom pain that often shot through his missing hand. He had rehearsed this moment in his head countless times, but as he hurried across the grounds of the Wolf's Lair, all he could think about was Keitel calling a sudden halt to the briefing, rushing to Stauffenberg's abandoned briefcase, shouting in alarm, evacuating the map room, calling for the SS guards to *find the colonel* . . .

Stauffenberg picked up his pace, rushing past the table beneath the oak tree. The Wolf's Lair felt like the ruins of some abandoned fort, desolate and decayed, but he knew that there were plenty of SS men and loyal officers residing in the various huts and bunkers. Any one of them could be idly glancing out of a window at the strange sight of Colonel Stauffenberg crossing the grounds alone, looking like he was going to break into a dead sprint at any moment.

He reached the signals shelter, a small wooden hut that looked like a miniature version of the map room. Inside, General Erich Fellgiebel, chief of signals at the Wolf's Lair, was hunched over his radio equipment. Fellgiebel's unruly black hair and thick spectacles made him resemble a slightly mad professor. His brilliance with systems of codes and top-secret communications made him indispensable to the war effort, but he hated the Nazis as much as Stauffenberg did. As soon as the bomb exploded, he was to telephone the plotters in Berlin, give the order to begin the takeover, then cut the lines at the Wolf's Lair, isolating the Führer's headquarters from the rest of the Nazi high command.

Fellgiebel blinked. "Is it in place?"

"It's in place," Stauffenberg confirmed. He glanced at a small round clock on the wall. The time was 12:40. He shook his head. "It should have gone off by now."

Both men stared out the window. The map room was at the other end of the compound, obscured by the forest.

"The mechanism is imprecise," Fellgiebel reminded him. "Be thankful it didn't decide to rush itself."

Stauffenberg held up his three fingers. "I might have lost another one."

His eyes darted from the window to the clock: 12:41. The silence in the signals shelter was unbearable.

"What will they say about us, I wonder?" Stauffenberg said.

"They will say that we did what we could, Claus."

"I fear that what they will say is, *we did not do nearly enough.*"

A single sharp blast ripped through the stillness of the forest. Stauffenberg felt a dull percussive *pop* deep in his guts, and the walls of the signals shelter trembled. Both men went to the window. There, above the canopy of greenery, a plume of black smoke curled up into the sky.

"Dear God . . . ," Fellgiebel said.

Stauffenberg knew that the plan called for him to spring into action. He had to clear the SS checkpoints before the guards locked down the compound. There was still the airfield, the plane to Berlin, the men across the Reich awaiting his commands . . .

But Stauffenberg felt like he'd stepped into a dream. So many years of planning, and now they had finally done it! Germany without Hitler—there was something completely unreal about that, so deeply had the Führer imprinted his twisted philosophy upon the country that Stauffenberg loved. As he watched the smoke rise and drift across the treetops, he thought of all the displaced souls who could soon return home from the meat grinder of this pointless war. He pictured the maps of France and the Eastern Front on the table in the map room, blasted into charred shreds, curling and burning to ash.

It was General Fellgiebel's words that tore him from his reverie. Stauffenberg turned away from the window in time to see the general slam down one phone and pick up another.

"It's done," he said into the mouthpiece. "Activate Valkyrie."

TWENTY-ONE

Max awakened in the dark. He was lying on a mattress. It felt like someone was driving an ice-cold needle into his brain. He kept his eyes closed. After a while, the pain dulled to a persistent, throbbing ache. He touched a finger to his face. There was a tender lump on his forehead, just above his left temple, crusted with dried blood.

Visions of firelight danced across the darkness behind his eyelids.

The smell of the ersatz fuel. The heat of the flames.

Boots on cobblestones.

A smirking boy, a silver pistol.

Eventually, he pieced the fragments together. He had been captured by the Hitler Youth. They were holding him somewhere dark.

"Gerta," he croaked. "Kat." There was no reply. He was alone in this place.

Hopefully that meant that the girls had managed to get away.

He drifted in and out of a pained, feverish sleep until faint light crept in through a small window set high into the wall. The window had been painted black, but a thin band of clear glass remained at its base. He found that he was in a room about the size of his bedroom in the safe house. Besides the mattress on the floor, the furniture consisted of a bucket and a single wooden chair. The walls were cement. Every now and then, footsteps crossed the room above. He was definitely in a cellar. After a while, he became aware of the smell of real oven-baked bread. How strange that something so comforting could invade this awful place!

Then he recalled the bakery next door to the Midnight Hunters' hunting lodge. That was probably "appropriated" from a Jewish shop owner, too, which meant that Heinrich and the Hitler Youth could use it for their purposes.

What those purposes were, Max had no idea. He sat up on the mattress, gritted his teeth against the pain in his skull, and pushed himself to his feet. He put out a hand to steady himself against the wall and waited for a wave of nausea to pass. Feeling his way along the wall in the near-darkness, he came to a door. It was locked, of course. He hadn't expected to walk out of this place so easily.

It could be worse, he told himself. The fact that he was being held in a bakery cellar rather than an interrogation room at Gestapo headquarters was probably a good thing.

Still, his stomach was knotted with fear. He was completely

helpless. He had lost his father's knife and managed to get himself captured.

He sat on his mattress and thought of Claus von Stauffenberg.

Suddenly, the door burst open to reveal Heinrich and the two heavyset Hitler Youth boys silhouetted in light pouring down a rickety wooden staircase at their backs.

"Get him in the chair," Heinrich commanded. The two boys yanked Max roughly to his feet and plunked him down in the wooden chair. There was no question of struggling or trying to make a run for it. Their grip was too strong, and he was still woozy from getting bashed in the head. As one of the boys held him by the shoulders, pressing him down on the seat, the other took a length of thin rope and bound his wrists to the back of the chair. Then he did the same with Max's ankles, binding them to the chair's front legs.

The two boys stepped back to flank the doorway, a pair of hulking shadows in the dim light.

Heinrich came forward. He was wearing a crisp, spotless uniform, but there was a smudge of dark soot on his face.

Claus von Stauffenberg would say something cavalier, something like *I heard you had a fire. I hope your clubhouse is okay.*

But right now, Max could barely picture the colonel, much less imitate his calm, collected demeanor. He could barely think of anything at all. His fear was black smog seeping into the room, wreathing his neck, slithering into his nose, burning his eyes . . .

He couldn't believe this was actually happening.

Heinrich leaned forward. Max flinched as the boy's face came very close to his own. Then Heinrich sniffed the bump on the side of Max's forehead.

"Smells like Jew blood." He frowned and thought for a moment. "Or maybe Gypsy. I get the two stenches confused." He straightened up and folded his arms. "So what is it? Jew? Gypsy? One of the subhuman Slavic races?"

Max looked away and stared at the wall. Heinrich grabbed his chin and turned his head so that their eyes met.

"Here's how this is going to work. I ask a question, you give me an answer. Otherwise, it goes very badly for you. Now." He let go of Max's chin. Max didn't dare look away. But then Heinrich clasped his hands behind his back and walked around behind the chair. Max's body tensed up. Not being able to see what Heinrich was doing was so much worse.

"What are you?" Heinrich said.

Max choked out a single word: "German."

"Ah," Heinrich said. "You see, that makes me very sad. Because the Jews, the Gypsies, the Russian dogs—they can't help what they are. But you are Aryan! You have the best blood in the world. And still you choose to fight your own kind, when we only have your best interests at heart. *That*"— he emphasized the word, made it bounce around the cellar's walls—"makes you a lower form of life than even those sub-humans." His breath came hot in Max's ear. "Because you had

136

a *choice*. And you chose to tear down what we've built. Do you think that was the right choice?"

Max clamped his lips shut.

"*Do you?*" Heinrich screamed.

Max felt his body begin to tremble. His heart hammered in his chest. He could feel Heinrich's looming presence at his back. Then, very slowly, the blade of his father's knife slid into view in front of his eyes. He lost control of himself and began to squirm and strain against the ropes. One of the heavyset boys laughed.

"Never mind that," Heinrich said. "Let's get down to business." The tip of the blade was so close to Max's left pupil that his eyelashes would brush against it if he dared to blink. "I want to know about the Red Dragons. I want the names of everyone in your group."

The knife vanished from sight. Max let out a long breath. Heinrich walked around the chair, returning to his place in front of Max. He knelt down, placed the knife on the floor at his side, and gently removed Max's left shoe. Then he picked up the knife and held the blade to Max's big toe.

Max screamed.

"I don't want to do this," Heinrich said. "Just tell me what I want to know, and I'll let you keep your toes."

"There's a hundred people in the Red Dragons!" Max blurted out. "I don't know their names, I swear!"

Heinrich sighed. He stood up, placed the tip of the knife

alongside Max's cheek, and flicked his wrist. The sharp, stinging pain brought tears to Max's eyes.

"I'm going to give you some time to think," Heinrich said. "Then I'm going to come back and start with your toes. If you keep lying to me, I'm going to take your fingers, too."

He sheathed the knife, turned his back, and stomped up the stairs. The other boys followed, closing the door behind them, leaving Max tied up and bleeding in the dark.

TWENTY-TWO

JULY 20, 1944

In the belly of the Heinkel courier aircraft, Stauffenberg tried to stay calm and focused. The first two phases of the plot had gone—miraculously—according to plan.

As soon as General Fellgiebel had given the order to activate Valkyrie, Haeften pulled up to the signals shelter in his staff car. Stauffenberg ran out and hopped in. On their way to the first checkpoint, they drove as close as they could to the map room. The scene was chaotic. Acrid smoke billowed from the wreckage, officers were being carried out on stretchers, and klaxon sirens were blaring across the Wolf's Lair.

The map room itself had been blown apart. To Stauffenberg, it looked as if it had suffered a mortar attack. The structure was gutted, and the remnants of its walls and roof littered the grounds.

"No one could have survived that," Stauffenberg said to Haeften as they sped past without attracting attention—just one more cog in the machinery of the bombing's frantic aftermath.

They had been waved through the first two checkpoints by SS officers who recognized Stauffenberg. The outer checkpoint was manned by a stubborn sergeant-major who insisted upon authorization from the Wolf's Lair before he would let them pass. But after Stauffenberg got out of the car and personally phoned the aide-de-camp of the compound, the final barrier was lifted. Haeften sped to the airfield.

The Führer is dead, Stauffenberg repeated to himself again and again. There was still so much work to be done if Valkyrie was to succeed, and yet—

The Führer is dead.

The man who brought evil fire down upon the summer fields of Europe had finally—and in a single instant—been wiped out.

He contemplated that for a moment, allowed himself a brief surge of triumph, then turned his thoughts to the work ahead of him. His brother Berthold and the other high-level coconspirators were waiting for him in the General Army Office at the Bendlerblock in Berlin. Now that Valkyrie was underway, it was crucial for soldiers loyal to the conspiracy to seal off the Bendlerblock to protect the nerve center of the operation from the Nazis.

Buckled into a seat across the Heinkel's cabin, which hummed and rattled with engine noise, Haeften looked pale. Stauffenberg shot him a reassuring smile, but the tension on the man's face brought to mind a stubborn truth: While the plane was in the air, he had no way of contacting his fellow plotters. He had to trust that they were proceeding according to General Fellgiebel's instructions. But until he was safely inside his office at the Bendlerblock, telephone in hand, he knew he would feel profoundly uneasy.

Three hours later, the plane touched down at an aerodrome just south of Berlin.

As his staff car wound through the streets, headed for the center of the city, Stauffenberg was relieved to find Berlin in a relative state of calm. That meant that Fellgiebel had succeeded in cutting off the Wolf's Lair from the outside world. If news of the assassination had already leaked, then Berlin would be under lockdown by the SS and Nazi checkpoints would be clogging the streets.

"Another mark in our favor," Stauffenberg said to Haeften as he pulled up to the stately office building that stretched from the Tiergarten to the Landwehr Canal.

Inside, the men made their way down winding corridors to Stauffenberg's office. Waiting for them was Stauffenberg's superior, General Friedrich Olbricht. It was Olbricht who had come up with the Valkyrie plan in the first place and recruited Stauffenberg to his office.

Stauffenberg greeted him warmly, but Olbricht looked grim. He rose from his chair.

"I've just heard from General Fellgiebel. The Führer lives."

TWENTY-THREE

Kat Vogel tapped out a fractured rhythm on her knee-caps. She barely realized she was moving her hands at all. Tension, sorrow, and fear drove the beat, while a grave sense of regret distorted the timing. It was jazz played by a band of maniacs as they walked off a cliff.

The radio was on, the German broadcasters' droning voices the background accompaniment.

The lyrics were provided by Ingrid and Karl Hoffmann. Gerta sat silently next to Kat, withdrawn, puffy-eyed, as sleepless as the rest of them.

"Tell it to me again," Ingrid Hoffmann said.

"We saw him run down to the other end of the street," Kat said. "When he lured the guard away, we threw the first bomb. And then we heard the footsteps of all the boys running at us. We left the other bombs where they were and got out of there."

"You're sure you didn't see him get taken by those boys?"

Karl Hoffmann said. His deep-set eyes looked impossibly weary.

"I'm sure," Kat said, reassuring Max's father for the hundredth time.

"Then where is he?" Ingrid said. "He's *always* come home before when he's gotten into a little trouble. Remember his first dead drop, when he thought he was being watched? Even then, he was back in a few hours. Now he's been gone all night and almost another whole day!" She rose from her seat. "I can't stand this waiting anymore, Karl."

"Nor can I," Karl Hoffmann said.

"I bet he's hiding out somewhere," Gerta said.

"Or maybe he . . ." Kat trailed off. She was trying to be helpful, but she couldn't think of where Max could possibly be. She thought he must have been captured by Heinrich and the Hitler Youth, but she couldn't bring herself to dash his parents' hopes.

She recalled the way those boys had tormented Gerhard in the community garden. They had hurt him badly—and he was one of their own. What would they do to a boy like Max?

"I'm going to look for him," Ingrid said.

"I'm coming, too," Gerta said.

"Me too," Kat said.

"You've done enough!" Ingrid snapped at her.

Kat felt her face flush. She looked down at the floor. Max's mother was right. It had been all her fault from the moment she threw the first rock at the Hitler Youth. She had been overcome by an urge to hurt those boys, and it had robbed her of her ability to think clearly.

"Ingrid," Karl said.

"Karl," Ingrid said miserably.

"Kat, it's not your fault," Karl said.

Ingrid sighed. She put one hand on Kat's shoulder and one on Gerta's. "I'm sorry. I'm to blame for this, not you. It's just that being here, in this place"—she glanced around the safe house sitting room in disgust—"has made me forget myself." She turned to Karl. "The last thing you said when we left our home, about how we're a family no matter where we live . . ." She shook her head. Kat was astonished to see tears spring to Ingrid Hoffmann's eyes. She had never seen her cry before. "This place changed something in me."

Gerta stood up and embraced her mother. "No, Mutti, we should have listened to you."

Ingrid held her tightly. "My little girl."

"And we shouldn't have come back here without him."

Kat felt Gerta's words land like an accusation. Her fingers and thumbs danced with hummingbird speed along the sides of her knees.

"I can't sit inside this house anymore," Karl announced.

"Let me come with you," Kat pleaded.

Karl pushed his glasses up the bridge of his nose and then paused, listening. He turned the radio volume up.

". . . has survived an attempt on his life," the broadcaster said. "I repeat: This is a special report. We have just received word that the Führer has survived an attempt on his life. Earlier today, an unknown assassin or group of assassins attempted to murder our Führer with what we believe to be a single bomb placed in a briefing room."

Karl's hand went to his mouth, then to a forelock of his hair. He shook his head in disbelief.

"My God," Ingrid said.

"The Führer is expected to address the German people later tonight," the broadcaster continued. "For now, let us be thankful that this cowardly attack has failed."

"Stauffenberg would have seen it through to the end," Karl said. "He would never have let Hitler survive."

"The Nazis are lying," Ingrid said. "They're stalling for time."

"No matter what happened, if the military is trying to activate Valkyrie," Karl said, "then the city will soon be at war with itself. The army will fight the SS for control."

"Then what about Max?" Gerta said.

"I don't know," Karl said. He ran a hand through his hair. "There's no way to know, unless . . ."

He went to the stairs and took them three at a time. Kat listened to him rush down the hall to his bedroom. A moment later, he came back down, looking bewildered.

"Ingrid," he said. "My trench knife is missing." He frowned, then turned to Kat.

"I didn't take it, I swear!" she said.

"Neither did I," Gerta said.

"You don't think Max . . . ," Ingrid said.

Karl took off his glasses and rubbed his eyes. "All right," he said. He crossed the room and sat down on the sofa. "Listen to me. I'm going to find him."

Everyone began to speak at once. Karl put up a hand and waited for the room to quiet down. Kat clasped her hands in her lap to keep from tapping out a jittery rhythm.

"I'm going alone," he said, "and that's the end of it." He turned to Ingrid. "If I'm not back by midnight, take the girls and go. Don't wait any longer. You know what to do."

"*Karl,*" she whispered. He stood up and they embraced. For what seemed like a full minute they held each other. Then Karl knelt down and pulled Gerta close.

"I will come back," he said, kissing her on the forehead.

"I love you, Papa," she said.

"I love you, too. I'm going to bring back your brother," he said. Then he took Kat by the shoulders and looked her in the eyes. She held his gaze.

"I'm sorry," she said.

"You have nothing to be sorry for. Your father would be proud of you. I'll see you soon."

With that, Karl Hoffmann put on his hat and left the house.

TWENTY-FOUR

JULY 20, 1944

Stauffenberg refused to believe that the Führer was alive. Nobody could have survived that blast. He had seen the wreckage of the map room with his own eyes.

Besides, Valkyrie was already in motion. Commands to begin the takeover had been sent out across the Reich. Paris, Vienna, and Prague had their orders. Urgent messages had been sent to Munich, Hamburg, Nuremburg, and dozens more key positions throughout Germany.

And now all of the conspirators were making frantic calls to the Bendlerblock office. Stauffenberg was personally answering them all, urging his comrades to stay the course.

"Yes. I was there, at the Wolf's Lair, and I am telling you—what you are hearing from the Nazi high command is nothing but propaganda. The Führer is dead. The SS and the Gestapo are to be arrested and their offices placed under military control. You have the full support of the Wehrmacht!"

While Stauffenberg took call after call, Olbricht and

Haeften bustled in and out of his office with reports.

The news was not good. No one had dealt with Joseph Goebbels, Reich Minister of Propaganda, and Nazi broadcasts had not been silenced as planned. Reports were being transmitted across Germany, assuring civilians and soldiers alike that the Führer was alive and well.

In Berlin, the commander of the city garrison refused, at the last minute, to order his troops to seal off the Bendlerblock. The conspirators were completely unprotected.

As night fell, gunfire erupted in the corridors of the General Army Office.

The SS had arrived.

Stauffenberg hung up the phone. He rose from his desk and looked from Olbricht to Haeften. Shouting in the hallways grew louder. There was another volley of gunfire. Someone screamed. A single shot silenced his cries.

"It has been an honor to serve with you gentlemen," Stauffenberg said, drawing his pistol. An eerie calm settled over him. For the first time in many months, he felt at peace. He no longer had to shoulder a vast conspiracy, or coordinate efforts across a multitude of cities. He had done what he could to topple the Nazis. His only hope was that his actions would inspire others to pick up where he left off.

"Perhaps there is still a way out for you." He pointed to the back door of his office. "The inner corridors may not yet be overrun. Find my brother Berthold and—"

"No." Haeften shook his head. "I began this with you. I will see it through to the end."

Olbricht drew his own pistol. "I suggest we pay a visit to General Fromm's office. I should like a word with him before this is finished."

General Friedrich Fromm commanded the Reserve Army. Though he had not pledged his full support, he had allowed the conspiracy to take root under his nose and had done nothing to stop it. He was the type of man who played both sides— reluctant to turn against the Nazis, but equally reluctant to distance himself fully from the plot to kill Hitler, just in case it succeeded.

Today, with the news that Hitler had survived, and Operation Valkyrie gradually appearing more and more hopeless, Fromm had announced that the conspirators had committed high treason.

They could no longer count on the troops of the Reserve Army.

Olbricht opened the door and stepped out into the hallway. Haeften and Stauffenberg followed. They moved down the corridor past the offices of men whom Stauffenberg had worked alongside for the past year. How strange it was to be hurrying with his gun drawn through a place where he had cheerfully gone about his business, asking after his fellow officers' wives and children, sharing a laugh on the way home after a long day.

The first shot came from behind them.

Stauffenberg whirled around, raised his pistol, and fired. The SS trooper at the other end of the hall ducked behind a bend in the corridor. A moment later, one of the office doors in the middle of the hall burst open and a pair of SS men fired at the three conspirators.

Stauffenberg felt a vicious tug in his shoulder. The impact of the bullet spun his body, and the gun that was perilously gripped in his three fingers clattered to the floor.

"Run," Haeften said, returning fire.

A dull, numbing ache spread from Stauffenberg's shoulder into his chest and down his arm. He wasn't afraid—the attack by the American fighter plane in North Africa had done much worse—but he knew the searing heat of the wound was yet to come.

He tried to run toward Fromm's office at the other end of the hall, but found that he could only stagger. Olbricht grabbed his good arm and pulled him onward while Haeften returned fire to keep the SS men pinned behind the door.

They reached Fromm's office and Olbricht kicked open the door. General Fromm had his ear to the telephone. When the two men burst in, he hung up and glared at Stauffenberg.

"I thought you would have put a bullet in your head an hour ago," Fromm said.

"I have no intention of shooting myself, General," Stauffenberg said. Each word sent little shock waves of pain into his chest and shoulder. Olbricht helped him into a chair.

Fromm shrugged. "It's over for you, either way."

"And you," Olbricht said. "Do you think Hitler, in his wrath, will let the commander of the Reserve Army live, after this provocation?"

Fromm paled. "I will personally deliver the traitors to him."

Suddenly, Haeften arrived in the room and leveled his pistol at Fromm. The general cringed and put up his hands.

"No, Werner," Stauffenberg said. "It won't accomplish anything."

Haeften scowled. With great effort, Stauffenberg stood up, placed his hand on Haeften's arm, and gently lowered it.

From the hallway came the sound of a dozen boots on the buffed marble floor.

Fromm smiled. "Gentlemen, welcome to your summary court-martial."

TWENTY-FIVE

The thin band of light at the bottom of the cellar's single blackened window dimmed, then disappeared. Max had been bound to the chair for several hours, and his shoulders were stiff and sore. His arms felt like blocks of wood.

The smell of freshly baked bread was a taunt, a reminder of better times dangled just out of reach.

In the first hour after Heinrich left him alone, his heart pounded uncontrollably. All he could think about was that huge blade hovering just above his toes.

When he was six years old, Max had sliced his arm on a broken signpost at the end of their street in Neukölln. The cut had been so deep, the sight of the wound made his knees buckle and his stomach queasy. The pain had been severe, but his father had patched him up and he had healed in a few days.

Now there would be no one to patch him up. Just the Hitler Youth boys grinning and laughing as Heinrich took his toes—unless he gave up his sister and Kat. Which would also mean that he was giving up his parents.

The fate of his family rested on Max's shoulders.

He knew that Stauffenberg would let Heinrich take all of his toes and fingers before he would betray his friends. But Max was more scared than he had ever been. He knew in his heart that the moment the blade sliced into his flesh he would be screaming the names of the Red Dragons.

He tried to move but only managed to make the chair hop slightly to the left. Anyway, the door was locked and there was nothing in this little room he could use as a tool to try and wedge it open.

Plodding footsteps came down the stairs. Someone heavier than Heinrich, Max thought. One of his henchmen, coming to deliver a quick beating before the real show began.

To calm his nerves he tried to breathe like his father had taught him. He vowed to withstand this, at least.

The door opened. Max blinked at the sight of a short, pudgy silhouette.

"Gerhard," he said, croaking the name from his parched throat.

The boy stepped into the room. He placed a tray on the floor in front of Max's chair. On the tray was a loaf of bread and a hunk of cheese. Then he turned to go.

"Wait!" Max said.

Gerhard hesitated. Then turned back. "What?"

"How am I supposed to reach the food?" He made the chair hop. "I can't move."

Gerhard shrugged. "Heinrich said I'm to put the tray down in front of you so you can see it. That's all."

"When is he coming back?"

"I don't know. Something's going on. The boys were mobilized."

A faint flicker of hope ignited within him. "What's happening out there?"

"Somebody set off a bomb in a meeting with the Führer. It's all over the radio."

Max wanted to shout. He controlled himself. "Is he dead?"

"No," Gerhard said. "He lived."

Just like that, hope was snuffed out. Despair, heavy as lead, crept into his chest. "Oh."

"I'm not supposed to talk to you," Gerhard said. But he didn't walk away.

"You did a good job, catching me," Max said, thinking quickly. "Heinrich must have been proud."

"He said I was one of them now," Gerhard said.

"Then imagine how happy he's going to be when I tell him what he wants to know, and I also tell him that it was you who convinced me to talk."

"Why would you do that?"

"Let me have some of that bread and cheese. I'm starving. I can't think."

Gerhard laughed. "I'm not an idiot."

"Just bring me the tray and untie my hands. Look"—he wiggled his feet—"keep my legs tied. I can't go anywhere. Then when I'm done you can tie me back up."

Gerhard looked from the tray of food to Max. "You'll tell Heinrich that it was me who got the names?"

"I'll *give* you the names personally, and you can tell him yourself. Just as soon as I eat."

Gerhard thought for a moment. "I'll untie *one* of your hands. That's it."

"Fine," Max said.

Cautiously, Gerhard went around behind the chair and fumbled with the rope that bound Max's right hand. Gradually, the knot loosened. Max pulled his hand free. His arm dangled at his side. He made a fist and unclenched it, then wiggled his fingers. Feeling rushed back, and then the pain came.

As soon as Gerhard set the tray of food on Max's lap, he moved as if to take the cheese, but grabbed the edge of the tray instead. Before Gerhard could back away, Max's arm shot up. He thrust the corner of the tray into the boy's neck, striking him just above the Adam's apple where his throat met his jaw.

Gerhard's eyes bulged. His hands clawed at his throat. Max lashed out with the tray a second time, catching the boy with a glancing blow to the side of his head.

Gerhard went to his knees.

Max dropped the tray, reached around behin

began working frantically at the knot that secured his left hand. He managed to loosen the rope, but not enough to free himself.

Gerhard caught his breath and lumbered to his feet. He stepped toward Max.

Finally, Max felt his left hand come loose. He picked up the fallen tray and flung it at Gerhard. The tray slammed into the boy's mouth. Gerhard squealed as blood spurted from his bottom lip.

With his arms free, Max found that he could stand up. He couldn't move very quickly with the chair attached to his legs. He had never punched somebody before, but he was fighting for his life. It wasn't pretty. He pummeled Gerhard's neck and mouth with backhanded blows, aiming for the places the tray had already struck.

Gerhard used his arms to shield his face and kicked out with his heavy boot. The blow caught Max on the shin. With the chair ruining his balance, it was enough to send him sprawling. Sideways on the floor, he managed to free his left leg. Gerhard came at him and he scuttled out of the way. As he moved along the wall, he untied his right leg.

Gerhard swung his fist and missed.

From the floor, Max grabbed a leg of the chair and hurled it as hard as he could. Gerhard brought his hands up, but part of the chair's seat clipped his ear and went crashing into the wall behind him.

Gerhard's spectacles went flying.

Max scrambled to his feet and ran for the door. Gerhard shouted and lunged for him. Max felt the boy's hand graze his shoulder as he darted through the door and slammed it shut behind him. He turned the bolt to lock it just as Gerhard tried to wrench it open. But all Gerhard could do was rattle the door on its hinges. Max collapsed against the steps, gasping for air.

He noticed for the first time that the door was made of steel. It muffled Gerhard's cries. Max shuddered. The bakery cellar was designed to keep noise in. He doubted he was Heinrich's first guest.

He took a moment to gather himself. He was exhausted and thirsty, and his head still throbbed from being pistol-whipped, but other than that he was unharmed. His left shoe was still inside the room. He took off his right shoe and left it in front of the door.

Cautiously, he crept up the stairs. At the top was a dim room full of metal racks where loaves of bread sat in neat rows.

He made his way through the bakery kitchen until he found what he was looking for: the back door. Outside, there was a small cement patio and a low fence that led to an alley. He trotted across the patio, hopped the fence, and headed out into the night.

It was strange being barefoot on the city streets, but he had never been so grateful to have all of his toes.

TWENTY-SIX

JULY 20, 1944

General Friedrich Fromm stood with his palms on his mahogany desk, regarding the conspirators seated before him.

Behind Stauffenberg, Olbricht, and Haeften stood five SS men with guns drawn.

"I assume responsibility for everything," Stauffenberg said. "These men beside me conducted themselves as soldiers, following my orders."

"Be that as it may," Fromm said, "high treason is high treason, and there can be no quarter given for an attempt on our Führer's life. Colonel Stauffenberg, General Olbricht, Lieutenant Haeften—you are hereby condemned to death." He raised his eyes to the SS troopers.

"Escort these men to the courtyard immediately."

TWENTY-SEVEN

The streets of Prenzlauer Berg were choked with SS checkpoints.

Thankfully, nobody paid any mind to a barefoot boy in filthy clothes. When one of the checkpoints proved to be unavoidable, Max cupped his hands, held them up to the officer, and asked if the man could spare a few Reichsmarks.

His family had been bombed out of their home, you see, and now it was up to him to scrounge up enough money to care for his mother and three sisters . . .

The SS guard waved him through.

It was almost midnight when Max walked in the door of the safe house. The radio was on. Gerta and Kat were on the sofa in the sitting room. Mutti paced the floor.

"Hello," he said.

Three heads turned. Three sets of eyes blinked. Mutti stared at him as if he were the Kaiser's ghost. Then she ran to embrace him.

"Maxi!" She smothered him with kisses, then studied his face. "My God!"

"It's nothing," he said. "I'm okay." He went to the sofa, where his sister gave him a suffocating hug.

"I knew they'd never get you," she said.

"They did get me," Max said. "But they didn't get my toes."

Gerta looked at his bare feet. "Um . . . I'm glad."

Kat approached him shyly. "I'm sorry, Max."

"It's okay."

"No, it's not. From the very beginning of all this, I let myself get carried away, and I put us all in danger."

"Without you, there'd be no Red Dragons," Max said.

"I'm just glad you're back."

"Did you see your father?" Mutti asked hesitantly, as if she didn't really want to know the answer.

"Papa?" Max said. "No, why, is he . . . ?"

Max looked around. His heart sank. "He went out, didn't he?"

"He's been gone for hours," Mutti said. "And with all this going on . . ." She gestured toward the window and the city outside. "I'm afraid for him, Maxi. It's no time to be out in the streets."

"What are they saying on the radio?" Max said.

"They're saying Hitler's still alive," Gerta said. "But we don't believe it."

"Well," Mutti said, "I think it's more that we don't know what to believe."

"He's dead," Max said firmly. "If Colonel Stauffenberg

planted the bomb, then Hitler has to be dead. He wouldn't screw it up."

Kat tapped out slow waltz time on the arm of the sofa. They all watched the hands of the small clock on the wall behind the radio.

"Midnight," Kat said gravely. Everyone looked at Mutti.

"What?" Max said.

"Your father told us to leave the safe house if he didn't get back by midnight. If he has been caught, it's too dangerous for us to stay."

"Leave and go where?" Max said.

Mutti sighed. "There are people who will help get us out of Germany. And eventually to Switzerland."

"*Switzerland*?" Gerta said.

Max thought of all the checkpoints in the streets—and that was just in Prenzlauer Berg. How would they ever reach the outskirts of Berlin, much less *Switzerland*?

"Mutti," Gerta continued, "even if we get out of the city, there's still all of Germany to cross!"

"Shh!" Kat said, turning up the volume on the radio.

Adolf Hitler's voice came over the airwaves. Slowly, Max sat down on the couch. He couldn't believe that Stauffenberg had failed, but there it was: the Führer's voice. It was shakier than usual, a little hoarse, but unmistakable.

"A small clique of criminally stupid officers have formed a plot to eliminate me. The bomb was placed by Colonel Claus von Stauffenberg. I myself sustained only minor scratches. I regard this as confirmation of the task imposed on me by Providence to continue on the road of my life—"

Mutti switched off the radio. "The Nazi crackdown will only get worse in the days to come. We're leaving Berlin tonight. Pack a bag. All of you."

She headed up the stairs, followed by Gerta and Kat.

Max sat alone in the silence of the sitting room. He thought of Papa, out in streets that were crawling with SS and Gestapo. He thought of Claus von Stauffenberg placing the bomb that somehow failed to finish the job.

Then he thought of the ruins of the Hitler Youth's clubhouse. It wasn't much in the grand scheme of the war—or even among the events of the past day. But it was a victory for the Red Dragons, and he would never forget it.

"I love you, Papa," he said, wishing the words out the window so that they might find him and bring some small comfort.

Then he closed his eyes and spoke to Stauffenberg.

"Good luck and God bless—wherever you are."

TWENTY-EIGHT

JULY 21, 1944
JUST AFTER MIDNIGHT

The headlamps of a staff car lit up the inner courtyard of the Bendlerblock. They shone across the neatly trimmed grass to illuminate a huge pile of sand, long and sloped like an ocean wave.

The condemned were lined up before this barrier.

Twenty paces away, half a dozen SS men stood at attention. An Obersturmführer called out names one by one, so that his men would know where to aim.

"Olbricht!" he yelled.

The SS men raised their rifles.

"Fire!"

The courtyard resounded. Olbricht fell. Smoke drifted through the headlamps' beams.

"Stauffenberg!"

The SS men aimed. Suddenly, Haeften lunged in front of

Stauffenberg, just as the Obersturmführer gave the command to fire. The bullets found him instead, and Werner von Haeften crumpled in the dirt.

Stauffenberg stood alone.

The Obersturmführer, slightly flustered, hesitated. Then he yelled Stauffenberg's name for the second time.

Stauffenberg took a step toward the rifles and shouted his last words—his allegiance to a country that had existed in his mind since he was a child roaming the forests of Lautlingen. A country with no place for men like Hitler. A country of freedom, justice, and honor.

"Long live sacred Germany!"

AUTHOR'S NOTE

The matter of Claus von Stauffenberg's last words is an interesting one. That he shouted *something* at his killers—some final defiant jab at the Nazis—has been confirmed by eyewitness accounts. Some say his last words were "Long live our sacred Germany." (The movie *Valkyrie*, in which Tom Cruise portrays Stauffenberg, uses this line minus the "our," which is what I've done.) Others claim his last words were actually "Long live our secret Germany," in reference to a poem by his hero, Stefan George. I chose the former for several reasons, mainly because the Secret Germany concept, while an important element of Stauffenberg's deep-rooted beliefs, is too complicated to unravel in this book and would have bogged down his point-of-view chapters.

Stauffenberg's activities in the weeks leading up to the final assassination attempt and the doomed Valkyrie takeover are fairly well documented. Wherever possible, I tried to place him in locations along with other people—mainly members of the Nazi high command—who were actually there at those times. Of course, the conversations they had, along with the thoughts running through Stauffenberg's head, have been entirely invented for this book.

Various aspects of the Valkyrie plot have been lightly fictionalized to fit the framework of this story, but the major details are rooted in fact. For example, the bombs really did rely on the broken glass/acid timer mechanism, which Stauffenberg had to arm via special pliers, and which made an already impossibly tense and complicated situation even more unpredictable. There actually was an aborted attempt that forced Stauffenberg to hurriedly disarm one of the bombs. Finally, none of the characters would have been aware of it at the time, but Hitler survived the blast at Wolf's Lair because the man standing next to him nudged the briefcase a little too far underneath the solid oak table. This was enough to shield Hitler from the worst of the blast and save his life. Thus, the tide of history turned on a man's shin.

As for the Hoffmanns, their adventures in this book are totally fictional, but not without historical precedent. The Red Dragons' Hitler Youth–fighting escapades were inspired by the courageous actions of the White Rose and the Edelweiss Pirates, two anti-Nazi resistance groups made up of German teenagers and college students. They distributed pamphlets, listened to American jazz (gasp!), and sometimes (in the case of the Pirates) ambushed Hitler Youth patrols.

The D-Day invasion and the beginning of the Allied march

across Europe correspond to the progress of the real campaign. Antony Beevor's book *D-Day: The Battle for Normandy* helped me keep those events organized. The announcement of the invasion and General Eisenhower's statement are both taken from the actual text of a radio broadcast.

ABOUT THE AUTHOR

Andy Marino was born and raised in upstate New York, and currently lives in New York City with his wife and two cats. You can visit him at andy-marino.com.

IN THE AFTERMATH, NOWHERE IS SAFE.
DON'T MISS BOOK 3: *ESCAPE.*

ANDY MARINO

THE PLOT TO KILL HITLER

BOOK THREE

ESCAPE

SCHOLASTIC